LAND OF MONSTERS

THE KIDS WHO DISCOVERED AMERICA

By Christian Darkin

978-1-9998930-5-7

First printing 2021

Rational Stories

www.RationalStories.com

About The Author

Christian Darkin is the author of more than fifteen books for adults, young adults and children. As a journalist in the UK, he has written on science and technology issues for newspapers such as The Times and The Guardian as well as dozens of newsstand magazines. He is also the journalist behind three science documentaries and the scriptwriter of a Doctor Who spinoff film. You can talk to Christian on Twitter at @animateddad.

Also By Christian Darkin

#Sharkgirl – a young adult ecological adventure
Lab Grown Meat Bites Back –a young adult sci-fi thriller
Deadly Placebo – an adventure in pseudoscience
The Skull – a middle-grade adventure
Act Normal – a series of chapter books for children

Thanks so much to Rachel for her amazing editing work on this book, for her encouragement, and for helping to bring it to the state in which you now see it.

Chapter 1

Djo had kept silent and that meant he was a coward.

He had known what had happened - but even now, two years later, he hadn't told a soul. Not his father. Not the elders. Not even the other children. He had allowed them all to think his little sister had just vanished - wandered off into the snow and not come back. He had watched the whole village searching. Helped in the search, calling out for her when he knew she would not be coming back. He had seen his parents grow more and more desperate as hours, then days passed, and hope faded. But all the time, he had known that Leal was dead and that it was his fault.

Every day since, Djo had choked that thought back, forcing it into the dark corners of his mind. But today he could not. Today was the day to think about the dead.

Djo turned the antler over in his hand, studying it for imperfections, and struck it at an angle, just the way his father had shown him, with the rough mammoth bone axe. The antler split, its end now a sharp white triangle like a raw, tooth.

"Making a spearhead," Djo's father had told the children as they sat around the fire, "means giving a part of yourself to it. What you think about while you work matters. The stronger your feelings, the stronger your work."

And what the children were making was no ordinary spearhead. "Tonight," Djo's father had told them, "is the night before your first hunt, and the blade you carve tonight is your Firstblade." He paused for effect. "It marks the start of your lives as hunters."

Djo had heard it all before, and he had been dreading carving this blade almost as much as he was dreading tomorrow's hunt. Thinking your own secret thoughts was as much a part of making your Firstblade as carving its shape was. And Djo could not deny it. His secret thoughts were about his sister, and the way he had let her die.

He struck the antler again, sharpening his point, just as the other four children around the campfire were doing with their own first attempts. Djo's father stopped in front of him, and pointed without expression at the uneven edge of Djo's blade. Leal had been his favourite. Djo swallowed hard, and ground the edge of the antler down with a rough stone.

They had been playing tag just at the edge of the village when it happened.

She was running, dodging between the tents when suddenly she froze, mid-laugh. Her eyes staring at something behind Djo's back. He turned and saw it. An ice-bear. It was forty paces away, Just black eyes and a black nose against the white snow, but he could tell it was huge.

And that was when the fear gripped him.

In a single second, the sight of the bear took his breath, and pinned him to the spot. Icy terror struck so deep in his chest it felt like a physical part of him.

The bear had seen them. It walked, head down towards them through the snow. Djo's mind was churning. There was time. Time to run. Time to call out, and bring the whole village shouting and hurling spears. He tried to force himself to move, but the seconds passed, and the bear moved closer and closer, and he could not even breathe. No sound came from his mouth. His legs refused to move. It was as though the bear had some kind of magic. He watched its approach, frozen in terror.

It was close now. Close enough to touch. Close enough for him to smell the sick, sweet smell of its breath. A mixture of wet grass, and dry blood. Icy sweat swept over his body.

The bear stopped, its eyes level with his face, looking straight at him, reaching deep inside his mind. Judging him for his fear. His cowardice. "Not yet," it seemed to say in a voice that came from within him. "Not yet," and then it slowly swung its head away. Away towards Leal. As though it had made a choice, a selection of her over him. Still rigid with shock, he watched it grab her like a doll, drag her back up and over the hill. And all the time, its eyes never left him. "Not yet," it seemed to say, "Not yet."

Why? Why had it not taken him? Why had he not been able to move? Those few seconds were frozen into his memory. The fear. Those eyes. That moment, frozen into his boots, when he realised that he could never be a hunter. And that guilt. The guilt that because he lacked courage, he had lived and she had died.

He glanced across at Ra, hammering impatiently at his piece of antler. They were the only children left now, the five around the campfire, carving their Firstblades. It would be so much easier, thought Djo, if the children could be friends. Ra looked up, and glared at Djo, silently mouthing the word, "Maker."

Djo looked back to his work. Ra had meant it as an insult. The reputation of makers was that they were weak, weedy, timid, cowardly. They spent their days carving and building with sticks and bones because they couldn't do anything else. Meanwhile, the rest of the tribe - the stronger ones who were able to hunt - brought back food for them, defended them, protected them.

"You wait till Djo gets a taste for the hunt," Djo's father always told the elders, "He'll forget all this. He'll get his growth spurt and he'll be out there with the best of them!" Djo's father was the best hunter in the village. He knew nothing else. But he was wrong. He was wrong, and Ra - stupid, bullying, hateful Ra - was right.

Djo was a maker. He loved the process of making tools. Reading the bone, chipping it, filing it, working it. He studied the tools of the village, the fire-making tools, the building tools, the sewing tools. He constantly asked why this was this way, and that was that way. Which mammoth bones fitted where in the structure of the shack that was his home.

How the skins were dried and prepared to make roofs and clothes. He watched and questioned and practised so much that the hunters had started to laugh at him. That was probably why Ra hated him so much. He thought too much, cared too much, felt too much, and he had no interest at all in what it meant to be a hunter.

If the hunts had been going well, that would not have mattered. There would have been a place for all kinds of people in the village. But they were not going well. Every year the ice got thinner. The rivers and lakes got wider. The sea crept inland. The land was changing and the mammoths were vanishing. That meant less of everything. Food, shelter, skins. The old were dying, and the young too, and now everyone had to be a hunter. Even Chi and Cha, the little twins, a boy and a girl, barely more than toddlers, would come on the hunt tomorrow. They played at carving their spearheads, seeing it all as a game, but it was no game. After them, no more children had been born in the village. Things had to change, and childhood was a luxury that could no longer be afforded.

Djo risked a glance up at Di - the last new hunter in tomorrow's group - and smiled half a smile in her direction. Slightly older than Djo, but far tougher, Di was a better hunter than him even before she had been on a real hunt. Not just a girl. Di was The Girl. The only girl left in the village except little Chi, and this gave her a strange kind of status amongst the adults.

They tiptoed around her like she was a precious, delicate snowflake. They watched her, talked about her. And especially they watched her with Ra. It was as though everyone was just holding their breath waiting for something.

This was odd, because Di did not behave like something delicate and precious. She behaved as though she were indestructible. She ran and fought, and day in, day out, she practised with a spear as though her life depended on it. Especially recently, thought Djo. Recently he would see her out at the edge of the village, stalking rabbits, or practising her throwing over and over again until the light failed. Djo worried a little. It was becoming an obsession with her.

Di looked up from her work, and caught Djo's eye. He looked away quickly. On the other side of the campfire, Ra was staring coldly at him. Ra made a stabbing gesture with his half-finished spearhead.

Between 12000-15000 years ago, during the Ice Age, when our story takes place, there was a bridge of land a few hundred miles wide between Siberia and North America. It was called Beringia. It was a cold and unfriendly land, bordered by ice, where saber-toothed cats and woolly mammoths roamed. Archaeologists have found bone tools showing that there were people living on the land bridge at that time, but hundreds of miles of icy glaciers blocked their way into America, and as far as we know, no humans had ever made it through to live in the Americas.

Life was already tough in the part of Beringia where our story takes place, but now the ice was melting, and as sea levels rose, Beringia itself was slowly flooding. This would have caused the tiny isolated communities of early humans huge problems. They would have found less and less food, and as the land shrunk and the animals living there vanished or changed. The settlements would have begun to die out.

Chapter 2

As Djo carved his Firstblade, past and present washed over him. His present, right there in the firelight, thumbs and fingers grinding and sharpening at the spearhead, every part focused on those tiny grooves and imperfections in the antler as he refined and refined it. His past, back there at the edge of the village. The ice-bear. The terror. The guilt. The knowledge of his own weakness. Was that what his father had meant when he had talked about your feelings when you carved your blade? Djo thought probably not. His father feared nothing.

His father had shown Djo his own Firstblade. He always wore it on a cord around his neck. Every hunter did. It was a crude piece of work, certainly, but that was the point. A hunter's Firstblade was never to be used. It was a landmark in the life of a hunter, a symbol of where you had come from. Each time you made another blade, you compared it to your first, and understood what you had learned on the hunt and in life. Where you started from was not the point. The point was how you grew.

Which was lucky.

Because he suddenly became aware that his father was standing behind him. The rest of the group crowded around. All looking down at his work.

"You going to play with that all night?" Ra laughed.

"Show me," Djo's father said. Djo slowly lifted the spearhead out of his lap. Afraid to show his work. Ra sniggered. Holding up his own spearhead, twice the size, its edges angular barbs.

Djo's father reached out a big, rough hand and took Djo's blade. His expression was unreadable. Was he disappointed? He flicked it over with his thumb so that the thin blade lay flat in his palm. He chewed his lip. The spearhead looked wrong. Djo was suddenly aware of every rough edge. Every fault in the material. Every misjudged uneven lump. He had thought he had a skill for this, but his Firstblade was a disgrace. He could see it now.

His father closed his fist over it, and, without speaking, stalked off to the big hut where the elders sat. Great. They were all going to see it now. Djo felt so stupid.

"Piece of rubbish!" said Ra. "Might make a toothpick."

"It wasn't finished!" said Djo.

Ra roared with laughter. "You mean you were going to make it smaller?"

Di and the little twins were looking on. Djo stood up and stared up at Ra.

The older boy stepped in closer. Ra was a stretched hand taller than him, and still smirking. "What?" he said.

"Leave him alone," said Di. Djo glared at her. He didn't need her to fight his battles for him.

He turned his head back, just in time to meet Ra's fist. A dull jarring pain shook him from the cheek down through his neck to his shoulders. He stepped back, dizzy, and shook his head to clear it. He would have a black eye tomorrow. He charged headlong at Ra's stomach, but the older boy was ready. His other fist, weighted by the heavy blade he had been carving, hit the side of Djo's chest. He staggered away, a sharp sting growing. He felt his chest, but his heavy pelt coat wasn't torn. There was a graze, but no blood. Ra at least hadn't used the point of his blade.

Djo straightened up, raised his fists. Ra laughed, and flicked his blade around in his hands. "Come on then, Maker-boy," he taunted. Djo tensed. Ra wouldn't use the blade, would he? Stab Djo right there in front of everyone? He wouldn't dare. But there was something in his eyes, thought Djo. Something in the way he held the blade, gripping it too tightly in the firelight.

The two had never been friends, but with every week that past, Ra was becoming more aggressive. More arrogant. More vicious in his taunts. Djo wasn't sure what he'd done to deserve Ra's hatred. But he'd noticed it was worse when Di was around. Maybe that was it. She was the only girl left in the village, and Ra wanted to be the only boy. "Teenage boys," the adults had laughed, shaking their heads in mock frustration. But this wasn't a joke. This was a boy with a fresh blade and eyes filled with a kind of madness that made Djo think he might use it.

The two boys stared at each other, Djo breathing hard. Ra grinning, beckoning him on. Surely he wouldn't...

Chapter 3

Djo's father appeared out of the hut and began walking towards them. Ra dropped his shoulders, and took a step back as though nothing had happened. Djo's father walked up, looked at him for a second and pressed the little blade into Djo's hand. For a moment he seemed to be struggling to say something. Then he cleared his throat, and spoke to all of them.

"Put your blade on a twine," he said. "Keep it round your neck always. Never use it." He paused. "Hunt tomorrow. Early." He strode off.

Djo wanted to cry. He wanted to throw his spearhead into the fire and start again. He certainly didn't want to wear the thing around his neck for the rest of his life. Ra pushed past him, heading in the direction of his family's hut.

"You should be careful," he said. "Hunts are dangerous. The weak ones don't come back." He held up his blade, shifting it in his grip.

Great, thought Djo. If Ra wanted to kill him and leave him in the snow, he'd have plenty of opportunity on the hunt. That was if Djo didn't get frozen to death, or taken by the saber-tooths, or lost, or trampled by a mammoth.

Djo crept off to a little dying fire where no other villagers were sitting, taking his time to thread his blade onto a leather strip and hang it around his neck. He made the thread long enough that the blade hung well down under his coat and out of sight. No point showing the other hunters what a poor job he'd done with it. As he watched the fire die, he longed for the time when he was as young as Chi and Cha. Back then, there had been children's voices all over the village. And women's voices too. Now it was just the hunters, and the few remaining elders. The whole place felt harder, harsher somehow.

By the time he made his way back home, most of the rest of the village was already asleep. As he passed Di's family hut, he could hear voices inside. They were indistinct beneath the wind flapping the thick mammoth skin walls, but it sounded like an argument. The only two left in Di's family were her and her grandmother, a hard, scary woman who seldom spoke except to tell the children off. She had seen too much, Djo had once heard her say, to ever laugh again.

Certainly, whatever conversation was going on inside the hut, it wasn't a happy one. Suddenly, the door flapped open and Di stormed out. Even in the moonlight, Djo could see that she was crying.

"Are you OK?" he said.

"What do you want?" Di almost screamed at him.

"I was just - " he started.

"Well don't!" she interrupted. "I don't need your help! I don't need any of you!" She strode off.

Djo pulled his coat tight around him. Away from the fire, the night was freezing. He made his way back to his own hut, and lay down next to the still warm coals and his father.

"It'll be all right tomorrow, won't it?" Djo whispered. "I don't feel ready." But his father was already asleep.

Chapter 4

Djo clambered out of the dark hut into the blinding morning. He blinked and tested his breath. It came out in a thick, white cloud so dense it was almost a solid object. "Breath is life," that was the old saying. The steam from your breath was what told you that you were alive. The stronger it was, the more alive you were. Grandfather Dran's breath had grown thin and almost invisible towards the end, shut up in the hut, huddled to the warming coals. Leal's had been a thick plume right up to her last moment when Djo had seen it drift into the air and vanish.

"You're not dead then!" Djo's father slapped him on the back, laughing. He had been up and ready for an hour. The prospect of the hunt always put him in a good mood, and Djo suspected that he preferred life out in the wilderness to the village. He couldn't imagine why. "The others are all waiting!" he said. "Come on." Djo followed him out across the white frosted mud of the path, between the steaming black rings of last night's fires and out to the edge of the village.

The others were not waiting. They were arguing.

"It's too dangerous," said Rok. Rok was one of the two elders coming along on the children's first hunt. Elder was a relative term. Neither he nor Phi was actually old, but the old, like the young, were a dying resource, and the village had to make do. "You should stay home and safe."

"Chi and Cha are going," said Di, "and they're only four!"

"That's different." said Rok, "You're -"

"I'm what?" said Di, "I'm strong. I'm good with a spear. I'm fast. I'm faster than you are!" She paused. "I'm a girl - is that what you were going to say?"

Rok didn't answer.

"I'm a girl!" protested Chi.

"But you little ones are just going to be watching the kill." said Rok. "She'll try to join in,"

"So?" said Di, "It's my choice."

"We can't afford to risk losing you," said Rok. "The village can't risk it."

"Why? Because I've got to have babies?" Di's face was hot with anger. Djo could see her breath swirling around her like smoke. She looked as though she was about to punch Rok in his lean, bearded face.

Ra stepped forward, "Everyone needs to learn to hunt," he said. "What happens when you're too old? Isn't it worse for the village if she can't find food?" Rok's eyes narrowed. "I'll look after her," said Ra.

Di shot him an angry glance. "I don't need you to look after me!" she said. "I can take care of myself. I'm a better hunter than Djo!" she said. She glanced over to where Djo was standing. "No offence," she added.

"I don't know -" said Rok.

Di grabbed a spear from the pile Phi was silently arranging as he watched the argument. "If you don't let me come, I'm going to follow you anyway," she said.

Rok was about to object, but Phi took his arm. Phi was older than Rok. He had never been great with a spear, but he knew how to read people, and he knew which battles were worth fighting. "Let her come," he said. His voice was quiet, soft. But something about the way he spoke made it clear it was more than a request. Rok shrugged, and handed out spears to Ra, Djo and his father. The twins were given their own spears - roughly pointed sticks, each about their own height - and they immediately set about battering each other with them.

The people of Beringia would have been experts at making the most of scarce resources, and the evidence they've left behind them indicates that they were a people entirely dependent upon woolly mammoths. They wore their skins, ate them, burned them, made weapons from them and built homes from their bones and skins.

The huts built by mammoth hunting tribes of Ice Age people have been discovered in still-frozen parts of Eastern Europe. They were usually created with the bones of many mammoths, with the jaws locked together to form walls, tusks formed into doorways, and several layers of hides stretched over them.

Some of the huts discovered are so big they could have housed dozens or even hundreds of people, and to build them would have taken the bones of many mammoths. These huts are thought to be amongst the oldest buildings ever found.

Chapter 5

The party left the village in silence, but Djo could feel the anger around him. Di was furious with Rok. Rok was ignoring Phi because he had overruled him. Ra was his usual teenage self, aggressive, arrogant and mean to Djo half the time - showing off to Di and the hunters the rest of the time. The only time he was happy was when he was showing off to Di by being mean to Djo.

Djo himself was miserable. Cold and miserable. That comment about Di being a better hunter than he was hurt him more than he wanted to admit. Not because it was true, which it clearly was. Not even because nobody questioned it. But more because she had said it. He wrapped the fur of his coat around him, and walked on, gripping the spear he secretly hoped he would never have to use.

Djo watched his father up ahead. He strode out in front, leading them away from the village as though he couldn't wait to leave. its busy, muddy huddle of huts. He probably imagined, thought Djo, that he was transforming his son. That in a couple of days, they would be back, dragging enough mammoth meat to feed the village for a month, and be welcomed with delight by the whole village. He probably hoped they'd have a story to tell too - some tale of bravery on Djo's part that would make everyone see that he was his father's son, and set aside all these taunts of "Maker" once and for all.

Djo knew better. His father was never at home long enough to see the truth - that Djo couldn't run, couldn't aim, and honestly just wasn't tough enough for the hunt. Djo cared about how things worked. How huts were built. How spears were carved. Using them just wasn't his skill. And this - this frozen trudging for maybe days and nights on end into the wilderness - was not what he was made for. If they found nothing, it would mean hunger and humiliation. If they found a mammoth - one hunter, two elders and a bunch of kids - well, what would happen next, Djo didn't even dare to imagine.

It wasn't supposed to be done like this, Djo thought. If the hunts were going well, being a maker would be fine. The hunters would still joke about it but they'd be glad the huts were secure, and the tools were well built.

But the hunts were not going well. Every year, the ice got thinner. The rivers and lakes got wider. The sea crept inland. The land was changing and the animals were vanishing. Growing up slowly was a luxury Djo and the others were not going to be allowed. They would have to become adults now. Right now.

It was clear how seriously the elders took the hunt when they decided that even the twins would have to come. They wouldn't be able to be at the kill, but they would learn to cut it up. How to use each piece. How to bind it to be carried back. Four years old and out on a hunt. However much they relished the adventure, thought Djo, this was a sign of desperate times. All the children - the whole future of the village - in one group. It was a massive risk by the elders.

Di, walking in front of him, turned suddenly to look back. For a moment, he thought she was looking at him, but her hood was pulled up tight around her face, so he couldn't see her eyes. As he passed her, he turned to follow her gaze back towards the village. The red sun was rising on a day of heavy clouds. The shacks built of bones and skins looked as though they were huge, hunched over animals. Mammoth tusks formed the arched entrance to each, like gaping toothed mouths. The whole village had turned out to watch them go. Hungry eyes hoping they would come back with something more than rabbits. Hoping they would come back alive. But amongst them, Djo spotted Di's grandmother. She looked more sour-faced than ever. Sadder. She nodded slowly at Di, who nodded back, then turned and walked on. Head down, hood covering her face. Breath escaping in a slow sigh, like steam from a cooking pot, winding into the sky.

Djo grasped his spear and thought of the stories, and part of him hoped they found nothing on the hunt despite the hunger in the village. He had never even killed a rabbit. Going up against a mammoth sounded like suicide.

He trudged on in the middle of the group. Ra had decided the hunt was on now. He stalked around the group, spotting movement in every clump of grass, his spear held constantly ready to throw. It would be funny if he wasn't so serious about it. The twins were behind, being hurried along and occasionally carried by the two older men. Di did not speak. She seemed lost in thought.

And so it went on for most of the cold, wet day.

The landscape was rocky and sparse. Each time they climbed to the top of a hill, Djo expected to see the landscape change on the other side. He wasn't sure what he thought it might change to - a lush expanse filled with wandering animals, perhaps. But there was no change. Low rust-red bushes and thick clumps of scratchy grass were spread thinly over black rock, and patches of snow lay everywhere. There was nothing to stop the cold wind, and no sign of anything alive. How the hunters came back with caribou or woolly mammoth from this wilderness, Djo couldn't imagine. There was nothing, and they walked on through it until his feet felt frozen and heavy. It was miserable. Djo had expected hunting to be cold and dangerous. He hadn't expected it to be boring as well.

Chapter 6

Suddenly, from the back of the group, a shout went up. Djo turned in time to see the twins running, full speed out to the left. They were bellowing excitedly at the tops of their voices, and waiving their blunted spears above their heads as though pursuing a wild beast. Some distance away, a pair of floppy ears perked up from behind a tuft of grass. The little rabbit, a straggly, thin thing that didn't look as though it would feed one of the twins, stared at the ferocious warriors, hurtling towards it. It chewed down its mouthful of dry grass, and then turned and hopped lazily away, its white tail bobbing after it over the hillside.

The twins broke off the chase, looking disappointed. Cha threw down his spear. It landed on his sister's toe, and she turned and pushed him over. He yelled, then started to cry. Then suddenly, both of them were screaming, and pushing each other.

Djo couldn't help laughing. Di turned, and looked up. She pushed her hood back and smiled. Suddenly she was running back towards them, breaking up the fight, hugging Cha and rubbing his bruised foot. "Come on!" she said, running off, laughing. The twins chased her. Djo watched. Maybe he had misread her dark mood. She looked happy enough now. "Look, a mammoth!" she shouted, pointing at Djo. The fur and skin coat draped over his shoulders was indeed cut from a mammoth hide, and he must have looked enough like a beast to fire the youngsters' imaginations because they instantly held up their spears and pelted directly at him.

Di was laughing and Djo shot her a look of pretend annoyance before galloping off up the hill, his arm swinging trunk-like in front of him. The twins were on him in a moment, leaping at him, jabbing him with their weapons. It actually hurt a lot more than he had expected, but he looked over to Di, who was loving it, so he grinned and went down on his knees. One of the twins - he didn't know which - dived onto his back from behind, raining down blows on his back, forcing him over. Soon the three of them were rolling down the hill together, laughing.

As he stood up and brushed the snow off his coat, and the twins tore off back to the group, laughing and cheering, everyone else was laughing. Everyone except Ra. Ra was just scowling at him. As they started to walk on, Ra pushed past him.

"Hunt's a serious job," he spat, "you probably scared everything off with all that!" As if you can scare off a mammoth, thought Djo. But he kept quiet. He didn't want another black eye.

The sun was getting low when they crested a hill, and suddenly everything did change. On the other side there was no lush grassland though, just ice and snow stretching off into the distance. The group caught up and looked down at it. In front of them, the earth was a wide border of scraped and churned mud and rock. Beyond that, about ten minutes' walk away, was a huge, rounded plate of ice spilling out between two hills, and beyond that, there was nothing but smooth rippling white.

The glacier. The Great Barrier, they sometimes called it. A high wall of ice, and beyond it a frozen nothing that went on, desolate, for what might as well have been forever. Out there, not a plant grew. Not an animal roamed, at least not by choice. Djo had never seen it, but he had heard. The Great Barrier was the edge of everything.

Djo's father, Rok and Phi led the group down the hill and across the mud to the edge of the ice. As they got closer, Djo saw that the edge was not smooth. In places, it was a low shelf, in others, a huge wall, four times his height. He put his hand on it. It felt like rock, but the way it was shaped, huge and round, was as though it had flowed down between the hills in a slow liquid. A little further along, the snow had fallen away, creating a gentle uphill path onto the top of the ice. As they came level with it, Rok put his hand up for everyone to stop, and the group crowded around behind him.

Djo peered past the adults who were pointing down onto the mud. It looked to him like a churned mess. Round puddles, about the length of his forearm, were stamped into the ground. He leaned forward, just in time for Ra to jab him in the back and send him toppling face first into the icy mud. Djo heard him laugh, and turned to see Di stifling a giggle. As soon as she saw him looking, she stopped and offered Djo her hand to help him up. He took it and grunted a "thank you" at her, brushing the mud from his face.

He glared at Ra who held out his hands in a gesture of fake, mocking innocence. Djo looked over at his father for help but if he had noticed, he was ignoring the incident. Ra made himself busy with the marks on the ground. The other adults were gesturing and pointing off along the edge of the ice flow.

"Mammoths," Di said to him. "A family group heading that way." Djo looked down at the ground. The round puddles were massive footprints. But there was something else. The steps weren't simply footprints leading along the edge. They were churned, stamped over each other. They turned in random directions. Here and there was a smudge where thick hair had been dragged through the mud, and occasional long channels. Scrapes where tusks had gouged the ground.

"Something happened here," he said, "before they moved off."

"That's my boy!" Djo's father slapped his back. "Now what was it?" Djo looked back at the ground. It made no sense.

"Saber-tooths?" he said without much conviction. His father shook his head. Djo felt his face heat up. Saber-tooths wouldn't attack a mammoth group. Not unless there were babies and the smallest footprints were four or five year-olds. Besides, there were no saber-tooth prints.

"Look." his father pointed at the snow. A single set of mammoth footprints, big ones, led off up to the top of the glacier. Between them was a little trail of blood.

"A rogue male," Di jumped in, "must have got into a fight with the mother. Wounded too."

"What are we waiting for?" Ra had leaped in front of the group and was halfway up the path to the top of the ice flow. Rok grabbed him and pulled him back by the coat.

"Eager to go out on the Great Barrier, are you? You want to meet him in the snow in the middle of the night?" Rok said. "We camp here, where we can find fuel for a fire. We wait until it gets light, and we can track him easy. Let him get tired and hungry - then we've got a chance."

Chapter 7

Back home, each family slept in a tent held up by bones, and insulated by thick layers of hide. The fire was inside, and a hole in the roof let the worst of the smoke out. It was dry and warm.

Djo had assumed, without really thinking about it, that when his father and the other hunters went out, they had some kind of protection against the weather and the animals. He had guessed that there would be clever survival techniques. Huts that could be instantly constructed and folded away. Shelters that the hunters could assemble out of things found in the wilderness.

The truth, he discovered, was that there was nothing. On the hunt you made do with what you found around you when it got dark. You grabbed what there was, and today, what there was turned out to be a shallow scooped out mud ditch, protected on one side by a wall of ice, and covered with a few hastily dragged bushes and the skins they were already wearing.

You lit a fire using more of the bushes, and a little seal fat and the spinner and bow they had brought with them for the purpose. You ate what could be scavenged - today it was two scrawny rabbits among the eight of them. You huddled around the fire, telling stories until you were tired enough to sleep, and you hoped nothing would come to eat you in the night.

The stories were the one thing that made the experience bearable. As the night got darker, the twins curled up beside the fire, their energy exhausted, but Ra was buzzing.

"I don't see why we couldn't have just gone up there and finished it off!" he said, pointing up onto the top of the ice flow where the wounded mammoth bull must still be wandering, looking for food.

"You don't know what's up there," said Rok. "Ice-bears will follow a wounded mammoth for days. So will saber-tooths if they're hungry enough. Could be anything up there."

"Huh," shrugged Ra. "We'd have been back before now!"

"Maybe we would," said Rok, "or maybe a snowstorm would have come up. Or maybe it would have got dark and we'd have found a cliff straight into the sea. Or maybe we'd have killed it and taken our time getting back, and we'd be lost now."

Djo gnawed on his rabbit leg, and listened. The kill had been boiled down in a pot of snow with a few of the tenderest shoots that could be found on the bushes. It made a thin soup, and when it was gone, the bones were picked out and shared among the children. The lucky twins had got the heads, and had scraped the brains and eyes out with their fingers, licking them clean. There was nothing on Djo's bone, but he chewed on it anyway. If nothing else, he thought, it would clean the bits out of his teeth.

Ra was still protesting that he could have led the troupe safely back off the ice. He would, he said, have simply followed their footsteps. The adults laughed and asked how he would Do that in the dark. He mumbled something, and sulked.

Djo glanced across to where Di was sitting. Her face was lit bright and yellow on one side, and deeply shadowed on the other. She was watching Ra as he spoke. Her expression was strange. Smiling, but distant. As though she felt that something was ending for her.

"What's on the other side of the snow?" said Di suddenly. The adults laughed.

"There isn't another side," said Rok, eventually. "It's end of the world."

"What do you mean, the end of the world?" said Di.

Phi poked the fire, and a shower of sparks drifted into the air. He waited until everyone was watching, and then he started to speak. His voice was quiet as though talking to himself. "When we kill an animal, what do we do?"

Djo shrugged. Phi looked round at Di. Her eyes were narrow. She was leaning forward. "I know!" she said.

"Show me," said Phi. He dipped into the clatter of bones in the bottom of the pot and handed her two pieces, one from each of the rabbits.

Di took them, and next to the fire, she carefully scraped out a shallow hole through the snow and into the ground. She took the little bones and carefully laid them in it. She looked up at Phi. "I need a spear tip," she said. Phi nodded.

"Why?" said Phi.

"When we kill an animal we have to bury a part of it with a weapon." said Di. She was reciting what she had been told - what they had all been told. But Djo thought there was something urgent in her voice. as though she needed to understand.

"Why?" said Phi again.

"We have to take responsibility. It's the only way to calm its soul." she said.

"Good girl!" He used his own blade to quickly sharpen another fragment of bone into a rough point. "Use this." He handed it to her. She laid the point into the hole, and covered it over.

"Isn't it supposed to be the blade that killed it?" said Djo.

Phi nodded. "When you're on the hunt you can't always do everything right." he said. "If we buried our best blade with every rabbit we'd pretty soon be in trouble. It's the thought that counts." He paused and looked at Ra. "If an animal dies and its spirit isn't calm, do you know where it goes?" Djo smiled to himself as Ra looked up from the fire. Ra's mind, what there was of it, had been off fighting mammoths in the snow. He shook his head, and shrugged.

Phi jabbed a thumb towards the wall of ice behind him. "Up there, the snow goes on and on. After a day's walk there's only snow in front of you. No plants. No animals. After a week, only snow. It gets colder, and darker, and if you go on, past the ice. Past the mountains, there you'll find them. Every animal that ever died un-calm. They're angry, and they're waiting. Over the ice, reborn in terrible rage in the Land Of Monsters.

"Oh no!" said Ra, waving his hands in fake fear. "Angry rabbits! Save me from the angry rabbits!" Ra didn't care much who he made angry. Spirits, elders, Djo. It was all the same to him. Djo wished the elders had let him go onto the glacier on his own. He pictured Ra wandering, lost in a snowstorm, being devoured by a swarm of angry rabbit spirits. In his mind, he made their eyes red, and their teeth sharp as pointed spears. Why not? it was becoming increasingly clear from Ra's behaviour that only one of them was going to make it back from the hunt alive. Djo had to hope that Ra's own stupidity got him killed somehow. Maybe a bear would get him. For a second, Djo hoped it would. Then his mind flashed back to that day at the edge of camp. Those black eyes. No. He couldn't hope that. Not even for Ra.

Phi stared back at Ra across the fire. His eyes were cold. He waited for Ra to be quiet, and then spoke so softly he could barely be heard. "My grandfather told of a hunting party that went deep into the snow. Twenty men, all great hunters."

Djo's face was red-hot from the fire but cold wind was creeping down the back of his neck like icy fingers. He looked out at Phi with Rok and Djo's father sitting either side of him. Their faces were set grim and hard.

"They came upon the edge of the ice after a long, fruitless hunt. Suddenly their leader saw a caribou standing up on the top of the glacier. They followed, but when they got up top, it had vanished. Not even a footprint remained. Then the hunter saw it again, further on, a hundred paces deeper onto the flow. The men followed, but when they got to where it had been standing, it was gone. Again, no footprints. Then he saw it again, deeper into the snow. Further from the edge. Standing, watching them. They followed it until nightfall."

"What happened?" said Ra.

"Nobody knows," said Phi. "They were gone for a month. Only one came back alive, and he was driven mad. All I know is that un-calmed spirits have to go somewhere. All that anger can't just vanish."

"So what is it like - a land of monsters?" said Djo, enthralled.

"Well, now, how would I know? You're welcome to go and find out, it's just up there!" Phi laughed suddenly and loudly, and the tension was broken. In a second, everyone was laughing. How would he know what was beyond the ice? How would anyone? "Bed now, everyone! In the morning, we hunt!"

Djo went to sleep thinking about the Land Of Monsters. What, he wondered, happened if a person died without their spirit being calmed? What then? What if it were a little girl, taken by a bear? What horror would she be reborn as in the Land Of Monsters?

Throughout history humans have come across barriers they couldn't cross. And usually when they've done this, they've invented monsters and gods to fill in the gaps in their experience. In the case of the people living in Beringia, the glaciers formed natural a barrier hundreds of miles wide between Siberia and North America. On the glacier, there would have been little hope of food or shelter, and nobody has found any evidence that humans ever made it through until the ice melted thousands of years later.

We haven't found any evidence of what the humans living in Beringia believed, but it wouldn't be surprising if they created legends and stories about what was on the other side of the ice.

Most of the time, when humans invent monsters and gods, their fears turn out to be empty. However, this time, as we will discover later, the land on the other side of the ice was all too real...

Chapter 8

Djo woke suddenly. It was pitch dark, the fire smelled damp and burnt but it was out. There was something in the camp. A shape, a shadow, or a sound. His mind was confused for a second. He couldn't be sure what he had sensed. Then he saw it. A dark hunched shape on the other side of the fire pit. It was moving stealthily.

Beside him, the twins were sprawled, utterly unmoving. Beyond them, the shapes of the adults heaved in slow breathing sleep. Djo watched the shape on the other side of the fire. It moved around the fire, hunched over. Too small for an ice-bear. Too quiet for a caribou. A lone wolf maybe, sniffing round the camp, scavenging for remains in the cooking pot. It wouldn't have much luck today.

And then the shape straightened, standing upright. A human! It - she - turned and took one look back at the camp. The moon reflected in her eyes for a second. It was Di, eyes wet with tears. Djo lay still, watching. She turned, gripping her spear, and walked into the darkness.

Djo slipped out of the camp and followed silently. He watched her in the moonlight. She kept close to the edge of the glacier, using its wall for cover as she crept away from the camp. Every so often, she paused, looking down at the ground. She was following the prints of the mammoth family. But why?

Suddenly, she paused, frozen. Listening. She turned. Djo flattened himself against the wall of the glacier, his face pressed against the ice. She seemed to be staring back, scanning the darkness. The ice on Djo's cheek started to melt with the heat of his body, running in trickles down his neck and under his coat.

"You can come out, Di said finally. "I know you're there."

Djo stepped out into the moonlight. "How did you know?" said Djo.

"You're as quiet as a mammoth," she said.

"What are you doing out here?" he said. "There could be anything!" She stood still for a long time. He could hear her breathing. It was uneven, almost sobbing.

"I'm escaping," she said.

"What?"

"I'm running away."

He thought he could hear her voice cracking. "From the hunt? You wanted to come!"

She shook her head. "From the hunt," she said, "from the village."

"But you'll die out here!" he said.

"Probably." he could definitely hear it now. She was choking back tears. "I'll die if I stay. At least this way I get to choose!"

"What are you talking about?"

"I'm nearly old enough to have children," she said.

Djo shrugged. "So what?"

"My mother died giving birth to me."

"I know," said Djo.

"And her sister died that way too."

"Is that what you're scared of?" said Djo.

"Since the hunger started, we're all weaker. It's happening more and more."

"You don't have to have children," said Djo. "You can be a hunter."

"Really?" she laughed, an angry, disbelieving laugh. "Djo, I'm the last girl! Do you know what that means?"

"No?" said Djo.

"You're supposed to be the clever one! It means if I don't have children - lots of children - then everybody dies. No more hunters. No more food. Everybody dies." Tears were rolling down her face now. Anger. Fear. Sadness. "Everywhere I go, I can see it on their faces: 'When will she be ready?' That's all they think about. I have to have babies, and I have to keep on having babies until I die. If I stay, then that's all I am."

"What will your grandmother say?"

"It was her idea," she said.

Djo thought back. Now it all made sense: the argument in the hut, Di's strange mood. "Where are you going?" he said. "You can't live out here on your own."

Di nodded at the ground. The mammoth prints were still there, a mother and five year old calves. "They'll be needing food. Mammoths know where the grass is. The mothers remember everything."

"So?"

"So where there is green, there is hunting," she said. "Maybe -"

"You're crazy!" said Djo, "I can help you!"

She shook her head. "You want to help me, don't let them follow me," she said. "Tell them a saber-tooth got me."

"I don't want you to go," said Djo. He was crying himself now. Despite the frozen night, he could feel his face burning. She must have known how he felt about her. She must have always known even though he had never said it out loud. Ra would have killed him if he had, so he just put it out of his mind. Now that it didn't matter, it was all he could think of.

"What difference does it make what you want?" she almost shouted. "Nobody cares what you want!"

Suddenly there was another voice. Another shape in the darkness next to him.

"What's going on?" Tt was his father. "Why are you out here?" he stared at the two of them.

A saber-tooth!" said Djo quickly. "It was round the camp - we had to-"

His father froze, scanning the darkness. "Where?" he said.

"Um... We chased it away," said Djo.

"Yes!" said Di. "We had to make sure it didn't come back."

"Good boy!" said his father. "You see - we'll make a hunter of you yet!" He slapped him on the back. "You two work well together you know." He gave them both a big smile, and a look that made Djo's face burn with embarrassment once more. "Come on - back to bed."

"Aren't you going to thank me for covering for you?" whispered Djo to Di as they followed his father back to the camp.

"Thank you? If it wasn't for you, I'd be gone!" She stomped off to the other side of the camp and curled up on the ground next to the twins. He watched her outline and listened to her breath. Only he knew she was crying.

He fought to stay awake to make sure she didn't try to leave again, but at some point he must have lost the fight, and the night closed in around him.

Chapter 9

"Come on! Up!" Djo's father was standing over him, reaching out a hand. Djo took a second to remember where he was, but it was the wet, cold mud that gave the game away, not his father's voice. He took his hand and was pulled immediately to his feet, still not fully awake.

Dawn hadn't yet broken, and his blurry eyes could barely make out the rest of the hunters in the pale grey light. His eyes cleared and to his relief, Di was there among them, gathering up her things, chatting to Ra as though nothing had happened. "Ugh?" he said, swaying slightly.

"Eager for your first kill?" his father was saying. "I bet you are!" He elbowed Djo painfully in the ribs.

"Yeah," said Djo, finding his spear and waving it vaguely in front of him in what he hoped would look like a gesture of enthusiasm, but, he felt, fell way short.

"OK, everybody, let's go!" shouted his father at the top of his voice, as he turned, spear raised, and marched off up the slope and into the snow. Ra pushed past Djo and stalked up onto the ice flow, surveying the wastes as though he was an experienced hunter.

Rok and Phi dragged the twins away from their giggling snowball fight, and followed, ushering the little ones ahead of them. Di lagged behind, looking back along the ice flow where the mammoth family's footprints lead away. When she caught Djo's eye, she pulled her lips tight and glared at him. A warning not to speak about last night. As if he ever would. What would he say? She stamped up the hill past him and onto the glacier.

Djo took one look back at the muddy camp and its rough bushes and burnt-out fire. Uncomfortable though last night had been, he had the definite feeling that worse was to come.

He trudged after the main group, his boots sinking deep into the soft snow. At the top, the ground levelled off, and Djo could see, for the first time, the landscape into which they were walking.

It was huge. Huge and alien. In front of him was a wide, flat, white plane. It stretched way off into the distance, and the rest of the group walking into it looked tiny. This endless, white blanket could swallow them all, and the mammoth they were tracking, and a thousand others, without leaving a single smudge on the landscape. Djo shivered. He didn't know if he believed the campfire stories, but he was certain this was not a place people were ever supposed to go. He might not be a born hunter like Di and Ra, but he had a fair idea of what it took to survive, and on this plain there was nothing.

At least Di wouldn't be making a run for it while they were up there in the wilderness. Even she wasn't that crazy.

In the distance the wide, red glow of the rising sun was picking out mountains. Djo couldn't tell if they were made of ice or rock. They could have been home to angry spirits or gods or monsters for all he knew. He stood at the top of the slope and looked out east over the terrible white.

OK, he thought, *here goes.*

The one good thing about all this snow was that the mammoth was easy to follow. Huge round pads of impacted snow led away, and between them, occasional spots of blood, red against the white. Here and there, there were churned-up scrapes in the snow where the creature had used its huge tusks to search in vain for grass under the surface.

Even Djo could have followed a track like that, and before long, he started to notice changes in the regular pattern of the footprints. He found himself walking ahead of the group, pausing whenever he noticed something odd.

"What's this?" he said to Rok. "See, one of the footprints in each set is sort of stretched." On the left side of the track, both prints were almost round. On the right, one was not. Every other print was shallower, and instead of being made up of a straight sided hole, punched into the snow, it was dragged out at the front.

"Well spotted," said Rok. "What do you think it means?"

Djo thought for a moment. "It's limping,"

"Yes!" said Rok.

"On the right, back leg!" Djo added, grinning. He'd got it right. By now, Ra and Di had caught up with them. Djo decided to push his luck.

"And it's slowing down, isn't it?" he said.

Ra stared at him mockingly. "How do you know that?" he said.

"Back there, the footprints were an arm's length apart. Now they're closer together," said Djo. "It's taking smaller steps so it must be slowing down."

"Good boy!" His father had joined the group and was looking over his shoulder.

"And I suppose you're going to tell me what it had for breakfast now!" said Ra.

"It didn't have anything - there's nothing out here!" snapped Djo.

Ra stomped off through the track Djo had been examining, obliterating it. "Makers!" he muttered under his breath.

Chapter 10

Even if the mammoth was slowing down, and limping, it had been walking all night while they slept, and the going was hard. Every step Djo took meant hauling his feet out of the thick snow, and crunching them back in. It was exhausting. Keeping his feet inside the mammoth's footprints helped a little because the snow there was already smashed hard, but it was still bitterly cold, and there was nothing - not a rock or a tree to stop the icy wind.

The ground rose and fell in drifts, and they followed the mammoth all morning, Djo struggled on, hood held tight around his face, head down, trudging.

Up ahead, Di seemed in strangely good spirits. Unable, at least at present, to run away, it seemed like a weight had lifted from her. He could hear her laughing and chatting with Ra and Djo's father, the three real hunters enjoying their chase while the elders herded the twins onwards. Djo felt tired, cold, out of place, and terribly lonely. It was a mess. It felt like things couldn't get any worse. Except of course, as he knew, they could, and almost certainly would. However great a hunter his father was, Djo knew that every step towards the white mountains was a step they would have to retrace on the way back.

Djo hoped the mammoth would change direction, but it didn't. Instead, it headed due east. Further and further from the edge of the ice flow. Further and further from home. Further and further towards the mountains and the spirits and the monsters. Djo tried to shake thoughts of the campfire stories from his head, but the memory of the fire's warmth kept dragging his mind back. It felt like that crackling fire was the last time he would ever get to be warm, and he could quite see how that party of twelve hunters had vanished into the ice never to return.

He looked at the distant mountains, and wondered if someone would one day tell stories of their party. They wouldn't, he decided. They wouldn't because their party was not twelve experienced hunters. Their party was just a group of children and elders.

Suddenly, the ground sloped up a particularly steep drift, and in front of him, Chi was being almost dragged up the slope by Rok who was losing patience with the struggling child.

"I'm hungry," Chi was protesting. She stamped her foot, wrenched herself out of Rok's grip and stood still, folding her arms. Rok tried to move her on, but she shook herself free and sat down in the snow, starting to cry.

"Come on," said Ra, "there's plenty of food this way. All we have to do is kill it!" He laughed.

Di looked down at the sulking child. "Come on," she said softly.

"No!" said Chi, "Won't!"

Di smiled. "Are you going to show me how you'll kill the mammoth?" she said.

Chi stared at her for a moment, caught between tears and pride, then leapt up. "Like this!" she shouted, and ran, yelling and laughing with her spear held above her head out past Djo at the front of the group, and disappeared out of sight over the top of the hill.

"You've got a way with them," said Djo.

Di spun round, glaring at him. "I don't like children. They get in the way," she said. But she was blushing, and Djo thought he saw a smile under the hood of her coat. Djo walked away up the hill, in front of the rest of the group. He kept looking back at Di. She was just so confusing.

When he did finally turn to look down the slope at where Chi was standing, Djo froze.

It was there, right in front of her. Its massive head, covered in matted dark hair, looking down, trunk swaying. Two huge tusks curved outwards and up from its mouth in a great sweep. Djo could see the end of one was encrusted with mud and snow and something that looked like blood.

The bull mammoth was a giant, even for its kind, and next to it, Chi, standing utterly still in the snow just a few steps from it, looked tiny. In her hand, her tiny toy spear was forgotten. The mammoth swayed slightly. Djo could see the movement of its muscles tensing under the thick, coarse hair, and at its right hip, there was a darker patch. Blood clumped the hair together in a dark liquid smudge. The mammoth stared down at Chi, and pawed the ground with its front leg.

Even Djo recognised the signs of an animal, wounded and angry.

Chapter 11

Djo was still taking the scene in when, from behind him, he heard a shout. It was Ra. He burst past Djo, bellowing at the top of his voice, and pelted down the hill straight at the mammoth. Djo thought for a second that Ra was trying to attack the beast on his own, but his spear was still strapped to his back. He held both hands out wide, and screamed at the angry creature as he barrelled towards it through the snow. Djo turned. Behind him, the others were looking on, horrified.

Ra was getting closer to the bull but he wasn't slowing down. He faced it, head on, still wailing at the top of his voice as he ran past the little Chi and straight at the creature's giant tusks.

The mammoth could have easily crushed him. One swing of its trunk. One step of its foot. One swipe of its sharp, bloodied tusk and Ra would be lying dead in the snow.

Instead, the huge bull, taken off-guard, took a sudden step back, turned and trotted away. Ra, seeing his gamble had paid off, followed, running crazily at the fleeing creature, but the retreat only lasted a few seconds. It stopped, turned, and faced Ra.

The boy skidded to a halt, spun round in a powder of snow, and fled back towards the group, the mammoth in pursuit. As he passed the still frozen Chi, he scooped her up and struggled back up to the top of the slope where Djo and the rest were standing.

The mammoth didn't follow. Instead, it paced at the bottom of the drift, unable, or unwilling to climb after him. Ra dropped Chi into the snow, and she began to cry.

"That was the stupidest thing I have ever seen!" said Rok.

" I saved her, didn't I?" shrugged Ra, still breathing hard, hands on his knees. "I knew it would run."

"You don't know anything," Djo's father had caught up with the group, and glared at Ra. "It could have killed you!"

"They always run if you surprise them." said Ra. "You said you've done it hundreds of times." Ra glared at him.

"See what your hunting stories do!" said Phi.

Djo's father rounded on Ra. "I didn't say they always run. Not the bulls! You were lucky!"

By now, Di was standing with them. She looked at Ra, still bent over, catching his breath. "That was very brave," she whispered. She put her arm out, and patted his back. Ra grinned at Djo, and shrugged as though it was nothing.

"It was dumb," said Djo under his breath.

"What would you have done, Maker-boy?" Ra stood up suddenly. "Oh, that's right, you didn't do anything!"

Djo didn't answer. Instead he pointed down at the mammoth at the bottom of the slope. It was pacing back and forth, glowering up at the group. "What are we going to do about that?" he said.

"It can't get up the hill - too lame," said Ra. "Just need to go down and finish it off." He shrugged, as though he'd done the main part of the job, and 'finishing it off' was something they could safely leave to the twins.

"Back right leg," said Djo, "just like I said."

But nobody was listening. The adults huddled together, and started scraping shapes in the snow, trying to figure out a plan. Eventually, they emerged.

"The three of us will spread out," said Djo's father, pointing at Rok and Phi. "you two go around behind it, and pin it against the slope so it's got nowhere to go. We'll finish it with the spears," he said.

"What do you want me to do?" said Ra, pulling his spear out and striking his most warrior-like pose.

"Stay here with the rest of the kids," ordered Rok. Ra plunged his spear into the snow in frustration. "Watch us, and maybe learn some teamwork."

The adults fanned out and made their way down the hill and around behind their prey. The mammoth watched them come. It was struggling, limping on its back leg. The fight with the other group of mammoths at the edge of the glacier must have wounded it badly, thought Djo. Killing it now would be the kindest thing the hunters could do. But he could see its breath rising in heavy clouds from its mouth. If breath was life, then it had plenty left.

Suddenly, the blunt end of Ra's spear hit Djo in the stomach so hard he doubled over. The pain was so instant and overwhelming it knocked the breath from his body. Before he was even aware of what was happening, Ra swung his spear around, and brought its blade sharply up to Djo's face. Ra's own face loomed in towards him, so close he could smell him.

"Don't ever call me dumb again, Maker," he said. Djo was so shocked he couldn't even speak. The blade was so close he could see its heavy crude barbs. He nodded feebly. Slowly, Ra let go and turned back to watch the hunters. As he turned, he whispered, "First chance I get, you're going to have an accident."

Djo swallowed hard. He was shaking. Ra was serious. He really did want to kill him.

At the bottom of the snowdrift, the mammoth turned to face its attackers. They formed a semi-circle around it. Djo's father stepped forward first, and the mammoth swung its head to face him. It put its head down ready to charge, and at that moment, the other two hunters leapt in towards it, jabbing their spears hard into its side.

The animal reacted instantly, rearing up, and stamping down with both feet so hard it felt like the ground was shaking. It turned and charged to the right, where Phi was standing. It had identified its weakest attacker. He backed away, and Djo's father saw his chance, launching his spear at the creature's side. The blade struck, but bounced off the thick, matted fur.

The mammoth turned back and forth as its attackers advanced, then, suddenly, it swung its huge shape right around, and charged directly up the snow drift towards Djo and the other children.

Ra reacted instantly, presenting his spear at the advancing animal, but the animal didn't even slow down, and from behind it, the three adults were yelling for the children to run. Di and Djo grabbed one of the twins each, and pelted to the left, down the side of the snow drift. The snow was too thick to get up any speed, and when he looked back, Djo saw Ra hurtling after him, the mammoth behind still charging, its feet throwing up huge showers of snow.

In a couple of seconds, Ra shot past Djo, shoulder-barging him as he went by, catching Djo off balance. Carrying Cha, Djo staggered, toppling forward, rolling down and down. Somehow he kept hold of Cha, as he rolled over and over down the drift. Shock mixed with fear - had that been deliberate? Did Ra really just push him under the feet of a charging mammoth?

He was spinning, but not slowing, in fact, he seemed to be getting faster, toppling over and over through the snow. He was sure the mammoth must be right behind him by now, and expected to feel its feet crushing him at any second. The snow was clinging to his clothes, squashing into the thick fur and piling thicker and thicker with each roll. He and Cha were turning into a giant snowball, growing bigger and bigger as he picked up speed. He held tightly onto Cha, shielding him as best he could.

Suddenly, there was nothing. The ground underneath them was gone, and they were airborne, spinning and toppling. There was the sensation of falling. It seemed to go on forever. He closed his eyes tight, and then they hit the ground hard, the snowball exploding around them. Djo felt his whole body shake, and for a second, the world was white spinning light. He shook his head and staggered to his feet. Cha was lying in the snow beside him. A few steps away, Di was sitting up, swaying from her fall. In front, Djo could see the ice cliff they had just fallen from. It looked impossibly high, and as he looked up, the figure of Ra ran, spear still in his hand, over the cliff. Djo must have overtaken him again as he had rolled and skidded down the slope. Ra was still running in mid-air as he crashed down into the soft snow. Behind him, in a great roar of snow, fur and tusks, the mammoth exploded over the edge. Scrabbling at the air, trunk and legs splaying around it, it pitched forward and plummeted head first into the ice, instantly dead. Around them, the ground shook alarmingly. Ice fell from the cliff, and then there was silence.

Djo looked down. Cha was still lying, face down in the snow. He could see his body starting to shake. Djo leaned down and hauled him up, expecting him to be crying. But he wasn't crying. He was giggling.

"Again, again!" he shouted. Chi was struggling out of Di's arms, running towards her brother, laughing. Djo looked over at Di, and then back at Ra, hauling himself out of the snow where he'd landed, feet sticking up. Ra waved, face breaking into a smile as he walked over. Di started to laugh, and then suddenly all the children were laughing helplessly in the snow, giggling together in relief. Ra even offered Djo his hand to help him up.

"No hard feelings," said Ra.

Djo blinked at him. "What?" he said. Had that push been an accident, and the threat just his idea of hunter talk? He just couldn't make it out. Djo's stomach still ached from the spear.

Chapter 12

By the time they had recovered, the adults had appeared at the top of the cliff. He could see them high above, relieved to see the children alive, but arguing amongst themselves. Djo couldn't hear what they were saying. Probably they were searching for a way down, or discussing how they were going to get the mammoth carcass back up the cliff and home. It didn't matter. The kill would feed the village for weeks. They could butcher it here, and take it back in pieces. It wasn't as though the meat was going to rot. Here on the ice, it would stay fresh for months, years even.

Then Djo saw the adults pointing behind him, and when he looked round, he knew things were going to be a little more complicated. He hadn't realised it before, but the platform they were standing on was, in fact, a ledge, perhaps a hundred paces long and fifty wide. The dead mammoth was in the middle, with Ra poking at it with his spear. Djo and Chi were on one side and Di was holding Cha close to the other edge. Behind them, the ground fell away as another cliff, and beyond that, ocean. The sea stretched in every direction, smooth and calm. Nothing, but a few huge white icebergs drifted in the distance.

He was stuck. Half way down a cliff with a dead mammoth a girl who wanted to run away, a possibly homicidal teenager and two four year old kids. Not ideal.

Djo looked up at the cliff face. It was vertical, but not terribly high. The face was icy and hard, but it was rough enough to provide a few handholds. Perhaps he could climb it? If he could get halfway, there was a little shelf. He'd be able to sit there, and maybe they could tie some skins together, and haul the little children up that way. Above, the adults could pull him up in the same way.

More importantly, if he could do it then he could prove something. That he was worth bringing along. That he had something to offer the group. That he wasn't just dead weight. It was worth a try.

He rubbed his hands, to get some feeling back into them, and walked over to the cliff face. He could feel Ra and Di's eyes on him, and above him, he could see the adults peering down over the edge, only their heads visible now.

He reached up and grabbed onto the wall. It was painfully cold, but the surface was pitted and hand-holds were easy to find. He tested his weight on it. If he was careful, he could do this. He reached up and grabbed the next hand hold. It was firm.

He lifted one leg, and felt for a lump in the cliff. Now he swung the other leg up, and kicked it hard into a snowy patch. There was a crunch, and his foot held. He reached up, then took another step.

"You can do it!" said Di behind him. Above, he could see a smile spreading over his father's face as he reached up towards him. The ledge was in sight now, just a few more footholds away. He felt the pride swelling in his chest. He could make it.

And that was when it happened. It started with the loudest sound Djo had ever heard. A rumble that could have been thunder if thunder came up from under your feet instead of high in the sky. But that was just the start. The cliff in front of Djo's hands shook. Lumps of ice crumbled from the wall and rained down around him. Not just fine flakes of ice, but fist sized rocks were dropping, bouncing off his clothes. He held on, and the sound subsided. He looked down and saw the cliff was rising. Somehow the ground beneath was getting further away. He gripped harder. What was happening?

He hung in mid-air, clinging to the wall. Under his freezing fingers, he could feel the whole wall shaking. He looked down. The ground was already a long drop beneath him. Di, Ra and the twins were looking up, shocked expressions on their faces.

Djo realised it was not the wall that was rising. It was the ground that was dropping!

He held on for a second longer, staring down. With a huge crash, which threw Di, Ra and the twins to the ground, the movement stopped. What was happening? Djo gripped as hard as he could to the wall. It was not shaking now, but vibrating, juddering like bone being scraped across rough ground.

He thought fast. Did he go up, and try to make it to the shelf, or down to Di and the others far below? Either way, the climb just got tougher, and the still shaking wall suggested that whatever was going on was not over yet.

In an instant, the decision was made for him.

There was a rumble, growing louder every second. The vibration in the wall grew with it, and a crack appeared along the bottom of the cliff. The whole shelf was splitting from one side to the other, detaching itself from the cliff wall. Djo looked down. For a second, he could see right down into the widening crack to the sea, far below. If he dropped now, he would fall right down into the crack. There would be no escape. Then the whole shelf rocked, forcing water up through the split at impossible speed, a blue white spray hurtling towards him between the ice and the cliff.

Instinctively, Djo, pushed himself away from the wall as hard as he could, throwing himself just clear of the crack as a huge fountain of water shot up through it. He flew through the air, and landed heavily in the snow on his back on the rocking ice shelf.

In a second, the fountain of water under pressure hit the top of the crack, and exploded in a spray which turned everything white and felt like needles of ice being fired into his exposed face and hands. He was soaked through to the skin in a moment, and lost in a freezing storm of icy salt water.

Djo scrambled to his feet, and looked up. As the white spray cleared, he could see the adults were now way above them, an impossible climb, but worse, the gap between the ledge and the cliff face was wider than he could jump, and it was growing every second.

The shelf had come away from the glacier. The children were now stranded on an iceberg, and drifting further and further out to sea.

Djo looked across at the adults. He could just make out the horror on his father's face, but there was no way back. The adults ran along the side of the cliff, following the children, but all the time, the gap was getting wider.

Djo, Ra and Di stared at each other in shocked horror. In the snow beside them, the little twins both started to cry.

Djo's father cupped his hands to his mouth and shouted. Djo could just hear him over the sound of the sea churning around the iceberg.

"We will follow you!" he was saying. "We will all follow!"

Icebergs are formed when glaciers start to warm, and pieces break off to float free in the ocean. The largest ever recorded was 31,000 square kilometres - larger than Belgium, but most are smaller - a few tens of metres in size. The one on which the children find themselves is a fairly average size, and would have contained about 150,000 tonnes of frozen fresh water.

Because of currents and winds, icebergs often follow a course which takes them close to the shoreline, but some can float out into open ocean where they melt. It takes an iceberg a couple of years to melt completely, but long before that, it can break up, become unstable, or tip over completely.

Chapter 13

Djo, Di and Ra stood on the iceberg and watched as the adults became tiny dots. And they carried on watching until the land itself vanished over the clear horizon. They barely spoke. The sea was calm and blue all around them. Finally, Chi tugged on Di's coat.

"I want to go home," she said.

Di looked back at her. "We can't go home tonight," she said.

"When?" said Chi. "When can we go home?"

Ra turned on her. "We're not going home," he said, "not ever. We've had it!"

"Shut up!" said Di, "Just shut up!"

"Well it's true," he said, "and they need to hear it!"

"Why?" said Di. "You're not helping anyone!"

"A hunter has to be honest!" said Ra. "It's the only way!" Chi started to sob again.

"Look what you've done!" said Di.

"We're all going to sit here until we die!" said Ra.

"We might drift back to land," said Di. "We might!"

Ra looked over at Djo. "What are you doing?"

Djo ignored him. He was studying the other pieces of floating ice. Some were lumps of their own iceberg, other, larger blocks must have detached from the glacier in other places, but all were moving one way. Eventually, he shook his head. "We're stuck in a current," he said. "We're not going back to land, we're going wherever the current goes."

"And where's that?" Di said. Djo pointed in the direction everything was moving. Out towards the western horizon. In front of them, the empty sea stretched forever.

Ra sat down heavily in the snow. "That's it then," he said.

"Maybe," said Djo. He walked slowly around the edge of their tiny floating island.

"What are you doing?" said Ra.

"Trying to look for anything that might help," said Djo without looking back. On two sides, there was a cliff straight down into the clear sea. On the other, the iceberg sloped more gradually off into the water. Around them, he could see no land. A couple of other larger icebergs floated some way off, matching their speed through the water, but they were too far away to have any chance of getting to them, even if there had been anything on them but ice. They were stuck.

Djo walked to the middle. The dead mammoth lay there, its tusks sticking up out of the snow, its head half buried. Blood had stained the snow deep red around it.

Finally, he spoke. "Well, we won't die of starvation," he said, patting the mammoth's flanks. The other two looked at him. "And we won't die of thirst. Plenty of fresh water here."

"Then we'll freeze!" said Ra. "There's no shelter, in case you hadn't noticed."

Djo's heart sank.

"Make a camp!" Chi said suddenly.

"We can't make a camp," began Di.

"Make a camp!" said Chi again, running over to the dead mammoth, and pulling at its fur. Cha joined him, climbing on the tusks.

"Let's make a camp!" he said. "Our house can be made of mammoth!"

Djo looked at the children. They were right. Back home in the village, the houses were made of mammoth fur stretched over bones and tusks. They were warm and secure, but making them was a grown-up job.

Di and Ra were looking at him, expecting him to come up with an answer. "I don't know how to do it!" he said.

"You watch them all the time!" said Di. "it's all you do back home!"

It was true. Djo had seen the adults take sun-bleached bones and hide, and weave twine to tie it all together. He'd watched, fascinated, as they hauled up the huge, curved tusks to form a doorway, and pinned back the sloping hide behind it. He'd asked them question after question about how the knots were tied and why each piece was fitted where it was. But seeing something done was not the same as doing it yourself.

And this wasn't a kit. It wasn't a carefully laid out set of pre-worked parts, ropes, hides, and bones all cut and prepared for building under the instructions of the village elders. This was a mammoth. A whole, huge, stinking, freshly dead mammoth. Where did you even start with that?

"I don't know how," he said. Ra rolled his eyes. "Well, at least I'm trying to do something!" said Djo. "You're just sitting there!"

Ra got to his feet and drew his spear, advancing on Djo. "There's nothing we can do!" he shouted straight into Djo's face.

But Djo wasn't going to back down this time. "You got us into this!" he said. "You made the mammoth chase us." Without thinking, he pushed Ra hard in the chest.

Ra staggered back and then recovered, a look of fury in his eyes. He levelled his spear. "I've had enough of you!"

"Stop it!" yelled Di. "Just stop it." The two boys faced each other, but did nothing. "If we want to have any chance, you two have got to work together." Ra's eyes were narrow, staring at Djo. His breath shot out in long streams from between gritted teeth. Djo watched it. He clenched his fists. Di stepped in between them, palms out to keep them apart. "Together! Understand?" she said.

After a long moment, Ra slowly lowered his spear. Djo relaxed his fists. They both nodded slowly.

Chapter 14

"Right, what tools have we got?" Di said, laying her spear down in the snow. Ra and Djo laid theirs down next to it. The twins joined in with their little pointed sticks.

"I've got this," said Djo, pulling out a pouch of fire-making tools - a spindle and a bow. It wasn't much to work with. Back at the village, there were tools for cutting, stitching and digging. Out here, they had just three stabbing blades and a couple of pointed sticks. None were designed for the job, but they would have to do. If nothing else, thought Djo, at least he could make fire.

"Well, the first thing we need to do is skin it," said Djo, looking over at the massive carcass.

"I've always been good with rabbits," Di said, as she got to work with the tip of her spear, "but their skin is a lot thinner." The three children started the gory job of dismembering the mammoth.

Di turned out to be quite an expert. The wound on the beast's back leg gave her a place to start, and in a few minutes, she had cut out a big rectangle of fur.

The other two dragged it onto the snow, and down the slope to the edge of the water. There, Djo instructed the twins to scrub it clean in the salty water. Then they hauled it back up the slope to dry in the sun. While it dried, and the skin became tougher and more like leather, the twins got to work on the next piece of hide Di had cut out.

Meanwhile, Ra and Djo got to work carving the meat from the bones. They started with the ribs, taking them out one at a time, scraping them clean, and laying them in the snow. Then they moved onto the huge leg bones, once Di had removed the skin, Djo sliced off the meat, and Ra dragged away the long, heavy bones.

They worked hard all through the day, wasting nothing. The meat that Djo removed was buried in the snow to feed the group for however long they stayed afloat. The thick white layer of fat around it was trimmed off and put to one side for the fire. The sinews were washed, salted with sea water, and then wound together into strong ropes.

Back home, Djo knew the huts were made mainly of jawbones, linked together to form walls, and held up by sticks. Here, that wasn't going to be possible. He would have to think of something else.

The huge head was too big and too heavy for even Djo and Ra together to lift - even if it could have been cut from the body, and they did not have the heavy axes they would need to do that. Instead, Djo decided to leave it just where it was, with the tusks sticking up, and use them to hold up the roof of their shelter.

At intervals leading away from the tusks, he and Ra planted the ribs deep into the snow so that they rose up on either side forming side walls. At the back, they heaved the huge heavy leg bones into position, and secured them in place with piled snow. They then poured water onto the snow. As it cooled, it would turn to ice, sealing the bones firmly into place.

Now, Djo used his spear to sharpen the ends of the twins' little sticks, and taught them to punch holes all along the edges of the sheets of fur, and then use the sinews to thread through them, sewing the furs together into a patchwork. It was tough, fiddly work for them, and their hands quickly became numb with cold, but Di managed to make it into a kind of game, and eventually, the work was done. The three older children worked together to drag the heavy, thick fur onto the bones, and drape it over the tusks to form a tent. They pulled it tight and secured it with more sinews, then they stood back to admire their work.

Chapter 15

"It looks like it's going to fall down," said Ra.

"It's not," said Djo, even though he knew Ra was right. It looked awful. Wet, lop-sided, lumpy. There were holes, and gaps, and one side was flapping alarmingly. "When it dries, the hide will shrink and the holes will close up. Always do." He said it surprisingly confidently. It was something he'd heard the adults back home saying whenever they built a shelter, but he was a long way from being convinced that this shack would stay up. "Come on, let's have a look inside," he said.

The children had to climb over the mammoth head to get into their new home, but once inside, it was warm and just about big enough for all of them. There was enough spare fur to line the floor with a thick, warm, soft carpet. This rug was a little smelly, and had rather more blood and rather more lice in it than any of them would have liked, but even Ra had to grudgingly admit, the shelter was a pretty good job all things considered.

When they ventured back outside, it was beginning to get dark.

"Food," said Ra decidedly. And nobody argued.

Ra took control of the fire building. He gathered some fragments of the mammoth bone, to build a fire, adding a little of the white fat Djo had collected. The little fire spluttered and spat with sparks of burning fat, but the flame was strong and long lasting, and all the children clustered eagerly around it as the stars started to fade in above them.

They roasted chunks of meat over the fire until they were charred and crispy on the outside, and rich and succulent on the inside. The smell of roasting was powerful, and Djo realised he had eaten nothing but a few mouthfuls of rabbit since they had left home. It seemed so long ago and so far away now. He dived into his chunk of mammoth, biting off huge, hot lumps, and barely chewing as he swallowed them. It tasted marvellous.

When he finally looked around, everyone else was gorging hungrily too. Their faces, lit by the yellow, sparking fire were dripping with sweat and fat, and they were the happiest Djo could remember having seen them since they'd left home. In fact, they were probably the happiest he'd seen them for a long time before that.

The children were not used to having enough food. For as long as Djo could remember, everything was rationed. A little of this, or a little of that each day, he was always told. This kill has to last for a week, or a month. The next meal might have been a day away, or a month.

He had vague memories of a time before the weather had changed, before the ice had crept back and the mammoths had started to vanish with it. Back then, there had been more children. Back then, he and Di and Ra had played together. Games of tag amongst the huts. Hunting games. Stories around the fire. Before the bear took Leal.

Ra and Djo had not been best friends - Ra had always preferred the rougher games, and was always quick to anger, but he had been devoted to Leal. Now that he thought about it, it was only after Leal was taken that Ra started to act coldly towards him. Perhaps Ra blamed Djo. Well that was one thing they had in common. Djo blamed himself too.

Whatever the truth, Ra and Djo had played together, and they had got along. Sitting around the fire now with full bellies brought back those memories in a sudden, unexpected surge. Djo wondered where those times had gone. Had it only been Ra who had changed, or was he different now too?

Maybe neither had really changed. Maybe all it took was a decent fire, and enough food to go around to make everything good again.

No, thought Djo. The group was in a terribly dangerous situation, but today, at least, for the first time in years, they could eat as much as they wanted and they were going to take full advantage.

When the feast was finally done, and everyone had stuffed themselves with as much mammoth as they could ever imagine eating, they put the fire out, and crawled inside the shelter, lying down on the soft carpet of fur, and falling satisfied to sleep.

Chapter 16

Djo woke before any of the others. It was a strange feeling to have the ground you were lying on swaying up and down, and Djo didn't like it. He stepped out of the camp, and went and sat at the edge of the iceberg. The sun was rising, and it was surprisingly clear and warm. The sea was empty all around them now, and everything was silent except the waves lapping against the ice, as they drifted onwards. Where were they? Djo wondered? They must be further from the village now than anyone had ever been. Even that lost hunting party that had wandered towards the haunted mountains must be way behind them by now.

"You're thinking about home?" It was Di, standing behind him. He nodded without looking round. "Maybe we've turned around. Maybe we're drifting back there right now," she said, hopefully.

"No," said Djo. He nodded towards the rising sun, "We're going East."

She sat down next to him, and sighed, her breath almost invisible as it was pulled from her to float out across the sea, as though it was her spirit being drawn back towards home.

"It's Ok for you," he said. "You like this stuff - hunting - I'm not cut out for it. I'd always thought I'd be the one to be at home and make the tools - learn to fish. This isn't for me."

"You're doing all right," she said. "We built a shelter, didn't we? We couldn't have done it without you showing us how."

Djo shrugged. "You'd have found a way."

"What are you talking about, maker boy?" Ra had stuck his head out from the tent and was blinking in the light. Back to his old self, thought Djo.

"He's trying to think of a way to get us home," said Di.

"Forget it," said Ra, "We don't even know which way home is."

"That way," Djo pointed back away from the sun. The sea was empty and flat right to the horizon.

"It doesn't matter," said Ra. "There's no way back. We're stuck here now!"

"Stop it," said Di. "They will follow us."

Ra shook his head. "How can they?" he said.

"They've got boats." said Di.

"Little canoes!" said Ra. "For fishing! Nobody goes out of sight of land, ever! You'd have to be suicidal. Anyway, they won't even have got back to the village yet!"

"You don't know!" shouted Di suddenly. "You don't know anything!" She launched herself at Ra, but he just twisted to the side, and Di went sprawling into the snow. She sat up.

"Nobody's coming," said Ra. "We're on our own." He skulked off to the other side of the iceberg where it sloped down into the sea. He stared into the water.

"They have to come," said Di to Djo, looking back towards home. "Don't you see it?"

"What do you mean?" said Djo.

"We're all the children of the village. Without us they've had it. They need us as much as we need them."

"I thought you wanted to leave," said Djo. "You were trying to run away before."

Di bit her lip. "I had to leave," she said. "That's not the same as wanting to."

"So you want to get home?"

"Yes! No!" She shook her head, confused. "It hardly matters now, does it?" She paused. There was that anger in her voice that she always used to mask tears. "Do you know what my grandmother told me to do?" Djo thought back to the argument he'd overheard in the village. Di's grandmother - the old woman who said she'd seen too much to ever smile again. He shook his head. "She told me the village was my enemy. That they would hunt me and not stop hunting until they brought me back. She said I had to treat men like I'd treat ice-bears. Run and hide if I wanted to live."

"She was always miserable," said Djo.

"She saw both her daughters die giving birth," said Di. "She just wanted to protect me."

"You really think they'll be following?" said Djo.

Di shrugged. "I had this idea, when I ran away," she said, slowly, "that if I followed the mammoths, they'd lead me to some green wilderness. Somewhere the hunting was good. Somewhere I could live for maybe a couple of years, until I was a bit older. A bit stronger. I thought maybe I could come back - when - when I was ready."

"That's mad." said Djo.

Di laughed. "I know. I thought I could come back, and lead everybody to somewhere better." She shrugged. "That was what I told myself."

Ra reappeared behind them. "What are you talking about now?"

"Boats," said Djo.

Ra shook his head, "I've been in those fishing canoes. They leak like anything. You have to spend half your time rowing and half bailing water out."

"Maybe you do," said Di. "Some people know how to fish."

"The only reason anyone goes fishing is if they're too dumb to hunt," said Ra.

"We have to find a way back," said Di. "Either that or we just sit here until we run out of food, or this melts." She picked up a handful of snow. It was starting to soften in the sun.

"She's right," said Djo. "We have to do something,"

"What?" said Ra.

"We can build our own boat!" Said Djo suddenly, although part of him knew he was only saying it to give Di some hope. "We can use some ribs to give it a shape - and if we strip the hair from the hide we can -"

"You're mad!" said Ra. "For all of us?"

"If it was big enough," said Djo, "we could make oars."

But Ra was shaking his head. "We'd all die!" he said.

"And if we stay here we'll die too," said Djo.

"Maybe we'll hit land," said Ra.

Djo pointed out towards the rising sun. "We're heading East," Djo said.

"So?"

"So, the only land that way is the Land Of Monsters."

"That's kid's stuff!" said Ra. "You still believe all that?"

"Can we really build this boat?" said Di. Djo nodded.

"I think so."

"You think so!" said Ra. "You THINK so?"

"What other choice have we got?" said Di.

"I'm not wasting my time building some stupid boat. We're better off staying here!" said Ra.

"Do it for the twins," said Djo. "What's going to happen if we tell them we're not going home? They're not going to just sit here day after day, we need to give them something to do - something to hope for."

"Even if it's a lie?" said Ra.

“Especially if it’s a lie!” said Djo.

Ra was about to reply, but Di didn’t give him the chance. She turned away from him, and strode over to the tent. She climbed up on the mammoth head that formed the entrance and shouted in to the two twins. “Wake up,” she said. “We’re building a boat!”

Chapter 17

The construction of the boat set the pattern for the days that followed. The children worked hard as a team, and followed Djo's instructions as closely as they could. But Djo himself was having doubts.

He tried to conceal it from the rest of the party, but he was becoming more and more worried. The boat had sounded like it might work, when he first suggested it, and Di and the twins had seized onto it as their best hope to get home, but the reality was a lot more uncertain.

Djo had studied how the adults of the village had made boats, and Ra was right. They were small - big enough for one person. They were unstable, turning over at the slightest wave, and worst of all they took on water at an alarming rate. So much so that before even being allowed to start learning their fishing skills, the children had been forced to learn to swim in the icy waters in case their boats sank. Djo shivered at the thought. Even in mid-summer, they could only stay in for a few minutes at a time before the cold started to eat away at them..

Then there was the fact that all the boats Djo had ever seen had been made from caribou skin, and strengthened with wood. That meant they were thin, and light, and easy to work into shape. Nobody had ever tried to make a boat out of a mammoth carcass and as the days passed, it became clearer and clearer why.

The children worked through the days removing patches of skin, pulling out the long, thick, wiry hairs, and then soaking, salting and drying, soaking, salting and drying the patches until they turned into leather - black, smooth and strong.

Once that was done, they worked on the bones, using the curved shapes of the ribs as best they could to shape a strong but hollow boat. But the ribs were thick and heavy. Djo sketched and re-sketched his design in the snow, trying to use as few of the bones as he could so as not to weigh the craft down, but at the same time, to give it enough strength to support five children against the sea.

When the work was done each day, and the rest were cooking, Djo sat watching the sun set in the west, looking for any sign on the horizon that they were being followed, but he saw nothing. Every day that passed, the iceberg drifted further East, and now it was turning South too. They had been gripped by a strong current and they were going wherever that current went.

The others were placing all their trust in him. Di and the twins were burying themselves in the work, eagerly rising to every challenge Djo set them. Meanwhile, Ra worked grudgingly. He could see as well as Djo could that the plan was a very dangerous one. Whenever he scowled and grumbled, Di shot him warning glances, and he quietened, but each day he was getting more angry and more frustrated.

Each day they were taken further across the empty ocean, and each day, Djo felt more and more alone.

Chapter 18

But there was something else, too. Something that pushed Djo to continue the work whatever he thought of their chances. The others must have noticed it too, and it must have been weighing on their minds, but until Cha spoke up, nobody dared to say anything.

"Are we dead?" the little boy said as they sewed the last of the skin into place on the hull of the boat. Di glanced nervously across at Ra.

"No," she said, "we're not dead."

"We must be dead," he insisted. "We're going to the Land of Monsters. You don't go there unless you're dead."

"The Land of Monsters is just a stupid story," said Ra. "It's not real."

"But -" said Cha.

"Ra's right," said Djo. "it's just a campfire story." Djo tried to sound as though he believed it, and most of the time, he did, but right at the back of his mind, the demons stirred. The un-quiet spirits of dead animals. They had to go somewhere. And that day behind the huts, when Leal was taken. There was something in the eyes of that ice-bear. Something that spoke to him inside his mind. "Not yet... not yet, but soon."

"But," said Cha again, "breath is life."

"Yes," said Di.

"I can't see my breath," said Cha, "and I can't see yours either."

The children looked around at each other. Everybody silently breathed out. The white steam that should have floated from their lips was gone. For the first time in any of their lives, they could not see their breath, and that, they had always been taught, meant death. Djo tried again. Nothing. He felt the air leave his lungs, but saw nothing. An empty hollow feeling spread from his stomach to his chest. He swallowed, and sucked in a deep breath, letting it out as slowly and gently as he could. Nothing again.

"It doesn't mean anything," he said, trying to convince himself. "It's just very hot here."

"But breath is life," insisted Cha.

"It's just hot weather. That's all. A bit of warm sun can't hurt us."

He tried a laugh, but at that second, there was a loud crash. An outcrop at the edge of the iceberg split away from the main island and smashed into the water. The whole iceberg rocked, throwing them all to the ground. They all scrambled up and peered over the edge. Tiny rivers of melting ice were trickling down the edge of the cliff. The iceberg was beginning to melt in the heat.

"Back to work, everyone," said Djo as brightly as he could. "There's plenty to do."

By the time the mammoth was completely skinned, Djo had all but given up hope. If he put it into the water, the boat would just sink. He was sure of it.

But then he made a gruesome discovery. The animal's intestines, a long, grey tube wound round and round inside its body, were starting to expand. They were the only part of the animal the children hadn't found any use for, but now Djo realised they could be the party's one chance of survival.

He explained his plan to Di, who grimaced, but then shrugged.

"We'd better get on with it, then," she said. Together, Di and Djo dragged the long, blue balloon of guts out across the ice and wrapped them round and round the hull of the boat. They looked disgusting, but they formed huge, air filled floats. The children had to work all through the day to bind the intestines to the skin all around the boat. But when it was done, and they all stepped back to look at their work, even Ra grimly agreed that it might just float.

That night, after the twins had been put to bed, the three older children sat around the spluttering fire. They all knew the boat was ready. They all knew that the sooner they left, the better their chances. They all knew what it meant to leave the relative safety of the iceberg to take their chances in the open sea. None of them spoke.

Right now, scientists are not sure how the first settlers got to America. Some think they somehow crossed the great glacier formed of hundreds of miles of ice between Siberia and Canada. As the ice melted, this would have become an easier journey, but it looks as though people had already arrived in America before the glacier had melted. Others believe they made their way around the coast, making short hops in primitive boats.

The iceberg on which Djo and his friends are floating is half-way between those two theories. Certainly the ice was melting at that time, and there would have been a lot of icebergs breaking off the coastline as the land bridge between Siberia and America slowly flooded.

However, it would have been a very dangerous journey for anyone trapped on a melting iceberg.

Chapter 19

The morning was bright. Di was first out of the tent, and when Djo joined her, she was already packing their few belongings into the boat. Mammoth meat for the journey, the spears. For water, she decided, they could tow a block of ice chipped from the iceberg behind them. She seemed bright and cheerful, eager to finally leave the iceberg, and start heading home.

Djo had a sinking feeling in his stomach. The boat had been his idea, but now that it was ready, he wasn't at all sure it was a good one. He looked back out to sea. A huge empty expanse. It was no rougher than it had been over the previous days, but somehow, now that they planned to sail out into it, the waves looked like a threatening and perilous landscape. stretching off into the distance.

The twins were next out of the tent, full of excitement. They couldn't wait to jump into the boat, and see what it was like to float on the sea. They probably loved the look of the waves. They probably thought they'd be back home by bedtime.

Ra stepped out of the camp. He looked dark and thoughtful.

"Come on!" said Di, brightly. "Help us get it down to the sea!" She eagerly grabbed the front of the boat, and started to drag it down the slope of snow towards where the iceberg sloped off into the water. The twins piled in to help, straining, their little hands against the back of the boat.

Ra stood at the entrance to the tent. He looked at Di and then at Djo. "You're really serious about this, aren't you?" he said.

"Of course we are!" said Di. "What do you think all this has been for?"

"We all know what it's been for!" Ra said. Djo watched them, staring angrily at each other. Di looked outraged that Ra was questioning the trip, but it was clear to Djo what he meant. He'd been half thinking it himself - that going back had never really been an option. That the whole boat building plan had just been an exercise to keep the twins busy while they waited for a sighting of some friendly land. That launching the five of them with a little water and a few handfuls of meat they had no way of cooking onto the empty sea in a boat they had no reason to think would even float was nothing short of suicide.

"How many days have we been drifting?" said Ra. "Ten? Twenty? And we've seen nothing. Not an island, not an iceberg. You want to try to row back all that way with not enough food or water? Even if you knew which way to go, you'd be rowing all day and all night against the current. In that?" He pointed at the rough, patched-together boat.

But Di was defiant. Enthusiastic, even. "We don't need to make it all the way back alone," she said. "You heard the hunters. They're following us. We're going to meet them."

"Of course they're not following us!" said Ra. "How could they be?"

By now, she and the twins had dragged the boat down to the water's edge. With one heave, she pushed it free, and suddenly it was floating. She grinned in triumph, and clambered in, followed by the two giggling twins.

Despite himself, Djo laughed, and ran down to the edge of the water. The boat was sitting perfectly. The skin was a perfect seal, and the inside was completely dry. The grey blue balloons of the mammoth intestines remained tightly bound to the sides, and kept the whole boat so high in the water, despite the fact it had three people in it, that it looked as though it could easily cope with the waves. He felt a swell of pride - this was his design, and it worked!

"Come on!" Di held her hand out for him, and he grabbed it and stepped in. The boat bobbed a little, but remained steady. He grabbed a bone oar, and tested it in the water. the boat floated forward. This might just work.

But Ra was standing, arms folded on the shore. "I'm not going," he said, slowly.

"What?" said Di.

"You don't stand a chance. I won't kill myself for your stupid idea."

Djo looked between them. Part of him thought that Ra was right, but how could he back out now?

In any case, Di had somehow convinced herself that this was the right course, and now she was going. She was taking the twins and going. And Djo knew that even if he thought it was the wrong decision, he couldn't just abandon them. He glanced over to Di. She smiled back at him, and he started to push with one bone oar, away from the ice. The boat rocked, and floated free. The twins cheered. Di put her oar into the water, and started to row. The boat pulled smoothly away from the iceberg.

Djo looked back at Ra, standing on the shore, unable to meet his eyes.

Chapter 20

"You're mad," Ra said. "You're all mad."

Djo couldn't argue with him. However safe it felt now, this was a huge risk. Djo felt the slight rocking of the boat, and was suddenly aware that they were floating in a thin skin of leather, alone on an endless ocean. Beneath the boat, the water stretched downwards to impossible, terrifying depths filled with - he really did not want to think about what could be down there.

Djo started to manoeuvre the boat around, getting used to turning it, feeling the weight of water against his oar.

At that moment, something in the water caught his eye. The sea was flat and slow. A dark blue that rolled gently by, its surface smooth out to the distance. But off in front of the boat, about fifty paces away, a ripple was growing. It was small. Maybe the height of his hand, but there was something about it. It was moving fast, as though being pushed by something big beneath the surface. Djo realised with a start that it was moving against the direction of the current, and towards the boat.

"What is it?" Di turned to follow Djo's gaze, but just as quickly as it had appeared, the wave vanished, sinking back down into the flat sea without slowing about twenty paces from them.

"Nothing, I guess," said Djo, not convincing himself. Di started to row.

Suddenly, a huge jolt shook the boat. Djo nearly dropped his oar into the water. Underneath them, he just glimpsed a flash of white hurtling at tremendous speed just below the surface.

"Get back here!" shouted Ra from the shore. He was desperately signalling to them - pointing out to sea. Standing on the iceberg, he was up higher, looking down on the water. He must be able to see what they couldn't. Djo dipped his paddle deep into the water and hauled it backwards, fighting against the boat's momentum.

"Look!" shouted Di. Out towards the side of the boat, two more waves were rushing in towards them. As Djo watched, he felt his heart jump. Behind each wave, a huge fin was rising. Not the short, wide fins of sharks. These were thin fins, black and shining, they rose out of the water almost as tall as Djo himself, and powering towards them.

He paddled frantically, but the boat was barely slowing its drift away from the iceberg. Djo cursed his own stupidity. He had thought the boat was moving easily because they were controlling it. In truth rowing was easy only when they were following the current away from the iceberg. Now they were fighting against it, the water foamed around their oars, and his arms burned with the effort, but it made little difference. They were still drifting sideways out into open sea.

To the side, the fins were rushing in now, and suddenly, one of them sank below the surface. Then the water seemed to explode. Something huge - as big as the boat itself - hurled itself high out of the water, flying through the air towards them, and then smashed back down, sinking below the surface. For a second, Djo got a glimpse of the tapering shape. The black and white patches on smooth, tight, oily skin. And those jaws - open wide and filled with curving white teeth. Djo's head and shoulders would have fitted easily between them. Killer whales! Three of them at least. And the children were sitting in a flimsy boat they could barely control, wrapped in the stinking intestines of a woolly mammoth.

The stench of skin and guts was powerful enough inside the boat. But Djo realised it must also be spreading out through the water, calling to every hungry creature in the sea. He had thought they were building an escape route. What they were building was a predator magnet.

The first killer whale hit the side of the boat hard, almost tipping them over. The twins were sprawled on the floor, their meat supply sloshing around them, covering them with blood. The animal dived deep, its tail flipping out of the water beside them, and catapulting a wall of icy water over Djo and Di into the boat. Djo grabbed the edge of the boat, struggling to avoid being thrown into the water.

There was a second before the next creature hit, head first, cracking one of the ribs which held the canoe rigid.

"They're trying to sink us," shouted Di. But this whale didn't dive. Instead, it raised its head out of the water right in front of Djo. He could see right into its huge, grinning mouth as the head lunged towards him. Without thinking, Djo jammed his oar into the creature's face, pushing as hard as he could. The animal swung its tail, forcing itself forwards at him, but Djo held on, bracing himself against the boat with his oar, and the boat itself started to move.

It was working. The creature, fighting to get to its prey was pushing them sideways back towards the iceberg.

"We have to turn the boat," he shouted to Di, and she immediately began to paddle furiously, swinging the boat around so that it cut through the water more easily back towards the ice shore.

Djo held on, but now his face was just an arm's length from the killer whale's open jaws. He could smell the rotting fish on its breath. See the tiny dark spot of its eye as it forced itself forward. The bone oar was bending. If it snapped now, he would fall head first into those jaws in a second.

But now he could see something else. Two, no three more tall fins were heading towards the boat. The iceberg was only a few strides away now, and the beast was still pushing them on towards it. There was no way they were going to make it before the three other whales hit. The twins were staring out, terrified, their faces covered in mammoth blood.

Of course, the mammoth meat!

"Throw the meat into the water!" he yelled at the twins. "Now!" Chi and Cha stared back at him for a second. Neither of them really understood what was happening. "Throw it!" he shouted again. Chi picked up a piece of meat and threw it out of the boat. "That's right!" yelled Djo, still fighting to hold onto the oar as the whale's face was pushing closer and closer to his own.

The other three orcas were nearly upon them, their huge heads rising out of the water as they rushed on. The twins grabbed a huge hunk of meat and hurled it out in front of the creature's jaws.

It worked.

The three whales descended on the meat, head first, dragging it down as they fought to tear it apart. Djo felt the front of the boat crunch into the beach of the iceberg, and when he turned, he saw Ra raise his spear, and hurl it directly at him. The spear grazed his cheek as it flew past, hitting the killer whale straight in the mouth.

The creature flipped instantly into the air and crashed down into the water. The spear dislodged from its mouth and sank out of sight as the creature powered away, leaving a stream of blood in its wake, and Djo and Di scrambled out of the boat. The three older children grabbed the craft and hauled it up the slope away from the water with the twins still rolling around in the bottom.

Gasping for breath, the three fell on their backs, their hearts thumping. Djo gripped the snow. It was painfully cold against his fingers, but he didn't care. It was safe and solid.

He sat up slowly, looking back into the water. The orcas had given up fighting over the mammoth meat, and were circling the iceberg.

A feeling of stupid guilt spread over him. He had known. He had known the boat was a dumb idea, that it would never work. And yet he had risked all of their lives because he had wanted to make Di happy. Had wanted to take her side, and leave Ra on the outside for once. He had been weak and stupid.

"I'm sorry," he said. "You were right, Ra. We should never have got in that thing!"

Ra grunted, his eyes still fixed on the sea. "I wasted a perfectly good spear on that," he said.

"Thanks for saving us," said Di.

"Didn't want to be stuck here on my own, did I?" he said.

"Yeah," said Djo. "Thank you."

"I was aiming at your head," Ra said. But under his hood, Djo thought he saw him smile a small, tight smile. What was he thinking? Was he proud that he'd saved them, or that he'd been proved right? Or was he just enjoying Djo's humiliation?

Chapter 21

The killer whales didn't leave. Djo watched them circling all through the day. There were six in all. The four adults that had attacked the boat, and two younger animals following behind. The injured adult was the leader. The stream of blood coming from its mouth had slowed now, but something in its movements showed pain and anger. The group must have been pretty hungry because they kept close. Every few minutes, the leader threw itself at the side of the iceberg, testing it for weaknesses. Each strike shook the ground, but there was no chance of it breaking up the floating island. As long as Djo and the others stayed out of the water, they would be fine, but the orcas were a constant threat, their dark fins cutting the water in silent patrol.

It was a hot day, and the sunlight was brighter than Djo had ever seen. The sea took on a green shade, and the light penetrated so deep that Djo could see the black and white oily shapes of the orcas even when they were deep underwater.

Di sat looking back out to sea. Chi and Cha wanted her to play, but she refused. She had tears in her eyes most of the time, but she refused to admit it. Djo knew it had only been the thin hope that the boat had offered of getting back to her family and the village that had been keeping her going.

With that gone, she had folded in on herself. She sat alone and silent all through the day and there was nothing Djo could do to reach her.

Ra, meanwhile, was insufferably cheerful. He strutted around the iceberg as if he owned the place. The only consolation was the fact that he had stopped, for the moment, trying to intimidate Djo. Whatever battle he thought was going on between them, he obviously thought he'd won it and Djo no longer felt as though Ra was plotting to tip him into the sea at the first opportunity. That was something, at least.

Djo tried his best to entertain the twins, but all the time, he was thinking. Ra might be happy that the boat had failed, but it was clear he had no other plan. Di was doing nothing either apart from staring, red-eyed, into the empty distance. And all the time, the iceberg was slowly melting around them. Everywhere, Djo looked, little trickles of water were escaping, flowing over the side of their little island in sparkling droplets. Djo watched them, a sick worry growing inside him. He reached his fingers to his neck, where his first-blade hung on its twine. It seemed an age since he had sat by the fireside carving it, with his father. He felt its sharp edges and wondered what help it would be against six hungry orcas in a strange empty sea far from home.

Chapter 22

It was half-way through the next night that it happened. A sudden crack of splintering ice shook them all awake, and Djo scrambled out of the shelter to see what was going on, with Ra and Di close behind him. In the blue moonlight, the white snow of the iceberg was split by a long, black zigzag from one end to the other. The heat of the sea had finally cracked the ice right through, and as the three watched, half of their iceberg silently fell away into the sea. They stared over the edge at it as it crumbled away, fracturing into pieces as it hit the water.

For a few seconds nothing happened. The three looked down the fresh cliff edge, dropping away in front of them. Then slowly, so slowly that it was a few seconds before Djo even became aware of it, the ground beneath their feet began to tip.

"The iceberg's turning!" Di suddenly shouted. Djo looked around. With the weight of the ice on one side gone, the iceberg was unbalanced now, and gravity was doing its work. The surface on which the mammoth carcass lay, propping up their camp was pitching backwards. They were now standing on a slope down into the dark, icy water, and it was getting steeper by the second. "The twins!" yelled Di.

At the bottom end of the iceberg, Djo saw their little boat start to slide towards the ocean. It picked up speed rapidly, and crashed straight into the water, bobbing away. Djo looked back. If the iceberg was tipping over, the camp, and the mammoth were going to go the same way in a matter of seconds.

He ran down the increasing slope, grabbed one of the huge tusks and swung himself inside the dark tent. The twins were waking.

"Grab me," he shouted, holding an arm out. Both children clambered up, and latched onto him, and he pulled them towards the entrance, still gripping the tusk with his other hand. He hauled himself back towards the doorway.

Suddenly, he felt the tusk jolt. The bindings above his head came loose, and the skin forming the camp's roof collapsed. At the bottom end, the huge bones supporting the tent fell away, and rolled down into the water. Djo felt the heavy pelt of the mammoth crash on top of him, but he kept hold of the twins.

He lunged forward and stepped up onto the mammoth skull, pulling the two children out from under the falling leather. The camp which had been their home was dragged away down the steepening mountain of snow, and was claimed by the ocean beneath.

Djo looked up. High above him, Di and Ra were struggling to hold on to the edge of what had been the freshly broken cliff, and was now turning into a mountain peak at the top of the iceberg. His mind struggled with the changing landscape, and at that moment, the mammoth corpse under his feet started to slide.

He acted instantly, dragging the twins with one arm, and reaching down into the animal's guts with the other for something to pull him up. As it slid towards the sea, Djo grasped onto something soft and rotting and hauled himself up, climbing, clambering and dragging with his free hand through the open and dissected remains of the mammoth. His feet slid on the blood. His numb fingers grabbed at bone and flesh and fur as he half climbed, half ran, up over and through the creature's rear until, just a moment before it crashed into the sea, he, and the twins made the leap from its back legs onto the snow.

But the snow itself was a near vertical face now. The two children detached themselves from his arms, and scrambled up it on their own. They climbed like spiders, hand over hand, faster than Djo could have walked, and in a few seconds, they had made it to Di's arms. Djo could see at the top of the slope, she and Ra had climbed over the cliff, and were now on ground which, though hard, and slippery ice, was at least, becoming more level by the second. If they remained straddling the raised corner of the iceberg, they could just about hold on.

His own position was bad and getting worse. He plunged both hands and both feet into the snow, hoping to hang on for as long as he could, but with every second the ground was getting steeper, and for all he knew, the iceberg would continue to tip until he was on the bottom, trapped in the frozen water under a mountain of ice. He could be frozen, drowned, or picked off by the killer whales. He held, grimly on and shut his eyes tight.

Slowly, Djo became aware that he had not hit the water. He was still hanging on, and the wall of snow and ice had stopped tipping. He opened his eyes cautiously and looked around. The way the iceberg had come to rest meant he was clinging to a perilously sloping cliff-face. High above him, the other four were looking down. Below him, the black ocean waited. What remained of the mammoth floated underneath him, and the orcas were devouring it. Their tails splashed the water, sending fountains of spray up as they powered into it, tearing off chunks with their huge teeth.

He hung there. No way down, and upwards was a sheer face of wet slippery ice. There was only one option. What had once been the uneven edge of their island was now a rough, angled blade leading up to the top. It wasn't quite vertical, and its edges had patches, cracks and jutting crags which might just provide foot and hand holds.

Gingerly, Djo lifted one foot and edged his way towards it. If he could make it there, then there was a chance he would be able to scale it. He took it slowly. One false move and he could lose his grip, and slide down right into the mouths of the killer whales. The corner seemed a very long way away, and his hands were becoming more and more numb with the cold, but slowly, step by step, he moved closer.

Finally, he was within grasping distance. He could see the edge was rough and broken. One more step and he could grab onto it. He had started to plan his climb up. He could see places for his hands and feet all the way up the slope. If he kept his nerve and climbed carefully, he was sure he could make it.

The last step from the snow covered cliff to the corner was the most difficult. He had to lift his foot high up and stretch across, to wedge it into a gap in the ice. Above him, the others could do nothing but watch. He slowly lifted his toe, took the weight on his fingers, and felt for the crevasse with his foot.

Suddenly, his foot slipped against the ice, and as he grasped tighter with his hand, the outcrop he was holding onto snapped off. He was hanging, with one hand and one foot attached to the wall as he swung away. He reached out and grabbed wildly at the only piece of ice he could touch.

It held, but he only had a second to steady himself and wedge his foot into the gap in the ice before a movement below made him look down.

Below him, the water had erupted and one of the killer whales was spinning through the air towards him, its huge mouth gaping wide. The mouth snapped shut, just a hand's stretch from his foot, and the shining black and white shape fell back into the water.

Djo grabbed onto the corner of the ice and started to scramble up, terror driving him on. Below him, the whale flipped over and dived. He could just see the white patch under its mouth deep under the water as it turned, and accelerated into another huge leap.

Djo reached up, dragging himself hand over hand, up the side of the iceberg. He wasn't even sure how he was finding footholds as he scrambled up, risking losing his grip with every step. The beast hurtled out of the water towards, him, falling just short, and crashing back down before circling round for another attempt.

This time, it was going to make sure. It left the water straight as a spear, hurling itself towards him. Djo's arms were heavy, his fingers, frozen sticks of numb pain as he jammed them into one ice crevice after another. As he lifted his back foot, he felt it bounce against something smooth and wet. He looked down. His foot was actually in the beast's mouth as it reached the top of its jump. He yanked it upwards just as the jaws snapped shut, and the creature fell away. Djo pulled himself up the final few steps to the top of the iceberg where the others were waiting. He collapsed, heart thumping, body shaking, emotion pounding through him in waves.

Chapter 23

The night was long and terrifying, and it was clear to Djo that they were only a little safer on the top of the tipped iceberg than he had been clinging to the cliff face. The five of them were perched on a knife-edge peak on what was now the top of the iceberg. There was no flat space anywhere on the slippery surface. The soft snow which had covered the flat side of the iceberg was gone now, and the whole surface was smooth sharp ice. Either side of them, the ice sloped steeply down into the water.

They had lost their shelter. They had no way of lighting a fire. Their food supply was gone, torn apart and sunk by the orcas. They couldn't even go to sleep without risking rolling off down the slope and into the water. Even worse, the ground no longer felt stable. They continually heard the cracking of ice deep within the heart of the iceberg, and every few minutes, there was a crash and a splash as another lump detached, and fell away. At any moment, the iceberg could split, or simply turn without warning. All they could do was hang on and wait for the iceberg to melt.

All night, they huddled precariously together, and watched the orcas playing in the moonlight. The whales were leaping out of the water, turning somersaults while they waited for their next meal to be delivered. It seemed they never rested.

When dawn did finally come, it was bright and hot. Djo could almost see the island melting underneath them. And just away from the remains of the iceberg, pulled along by the same drifting current, the children could see their little boat bobbing, softly on the smooth water. It had survived the slide into the sea, and now sat invitingly just a hundred paces or so away, if Djo could walk on water.

The orcas were still there. Breaking the crystal clear blue water with their backs, but they had lost interest in the boat. Instead, they followed, lazily circling the iceberg, as it drifted in the empty sea.

The children miserably watched the sun rise. Djo chipped away at the top of the iceberg with his spear, in the hope of leveling out a place where they might be able to lay down, one at a time and sleep for a few minutes, but it was hopeless. The twins drifted into a fitful sleep in Di's arms. She held them close, but Djo could tell she was thinking hard. Eventually she whispered to Ra:

"We need to make it quick for the little ones."

Djo looked at her in horror. "What are you talking about?" he said.

"I don't want the orcas to get them," she said. In the yellow sunrise, her face was half-lit. It looked like stone.

"I understand," Ra said grimly. "If the ice starts to turn, leave it to me."

"No!" said Djo. "There must be something we can do."

"Like what?" said Ra. "You want to make a boat from ice? Being clever won't help now. Face it, we're out of options."

"Where are we going to go now?" said Chi, shaking herself suddenly awake. The bigger children shifted nervously, nobody willing to say. They all looked out at the rising sun.

"Why don't we go and play on the beach?" said Cha, his eyes flicking open. He spoke so brightly that Di laughed, despite herself.

Suddenly she stopped, dead silent. Her expression changed. Cha was pointing out to sea away from the sunrise, and Di was staring out in the same direction. Djo turned. For a moment, he was still blinded by the bright light of the dawn they had all been intently watching. Then, slowly, his vision cleared, and he saw it.

His heart jumped. "Land!" he gasped. "Land!" They'd all been so desperately watching the sun rising that nobody had even looked in the direction the iceberg was drifting, and now that they did, they could see a clear line of yellow sand, and broken rust-coloured rocks, and above it a deep, dark green land sloping away and up towards even darker green hills, so high that their tops were lost in shaded white cloud.

Chapter 24

The children started, hope growing, then slowly, one by one, they turned to look at each other. Checking in each other's expressions that what they were seeing was real. Suddenly, there was laughter. They were all laughing. Joy. Relief. Hope. An explosion of emotions wrapped around Djo as he sat on the summit of the upturned iceberg, watching the band of land grow wider and stronger in front of them.

Djo had never seen a landscape so lush. Grey brown mud and dirt, scrubby ice-burnt bushes, and dirty snow were all he knew. Back home, trees were rare things, stranded and alone, their leaves blown by bitter winds. But now, as they drifted closer, they realised they could see thousands. Every mountain sprung with thickly-packed tall trees, and where they broke, yellow-green grass was everywhere.

Soon, the land was close enough that they could pick out the rocks on the shore, and see the lines of white where the waves were breaking.

By the time the sun was full, they could see the individual leaves on the trees. Birds sat in the branches welcoming them. It was too good to be true. The iceberg seemed to be carrying them right up to deposit them on the shore!

As the others continued to celebrate, Djo looked down into the water below them. It was blue green and clear. Far below them, the beach must stretch underneath the iceberg out into the ocean. Something was bothering him, but he wasn't sure what it was. He watched as the beach drew closer. The water under the iceberg was changing, the colour becoming lighter, more yellow.

He started to see white shapes, shoals of fish, scattering as they sailed towards the shore, and underneath, darker shapes. Rocks.

Rocks!

"Hold on!" he shouted.

There was a huge jolt. A grinding vibration shook through the iceberg and the entire thing tipped suddenly as it crashed to a grating, grinding halt on the reef below them. The five children grabbed each other. Ra was pitched forward, and lost his balance. His hand flailed, and he caught hold of Di. Djo grabbed Di, and the twins clung to her clothes as she scrabbled to stay upright.

Djo just had time to pull out his spear with his other hand, and drive its barbed point deep into a gap in the ice. For a second, the children swung in a long line, held from falling into the water only by Djo's grip on his spear. Then Di grabbed the corner of the iceberg, and together, they hauled themselves back up.

They looked out. The shore was, perhaps a couple of hundred paces away. It looked warm, dry and enticing. But between them and it was open water. And in the water were the orcas.

The killer whales were not paying attention. They were some way off, behind the iceberg. Djo could see their tails cutting the water.

"We can make it," said Di.

"Not a chance," said Djo. "They'd catch us before we got half-way."

"Maybe you," said Ra. "I reckon I could make it!"

"And the twins?" said Djo. "What chance would they have?"

"What, then?" Di said.

Djo looked around for an answer. "The boat!" he said. Their little mammoth skin boat had been drifting just behind, with the same current as the iceberg since it was tipped into the sea. The iceberg was grounded, but the boat was still floating freely somewhere between the orcas and them.

"What good is that?" said Ra. "We'd never get to it!" As they watched, the little boat continued to bob in the waves. "We should try for the shore - maybe some of us will make it!"

"It's coming this way," said Di. "Maybe if we wait?"

They watched. The boat floated a little closer. It was nearly within reach. Djo started to think it might be carried right to them, but then, caught in the current, it started to turn. Djo studied the waves. He shook his head.

"Look at the way the water is flowing." He pointed along the ridge of ripples forming the current. They led parallel to the beach for some distance, and then out to sea again. In a few seconds, the boat would be dragged away from them again. "There's no chance," he said. "It's being pulled away!"

"Then it has to be now," said Di.

"We should just go for the shore," said Ra, "There's a chance it's too shallow for them. We might make it."

Di hugged the children close to her. "I'm not risking them," she said.

"I'm fed up with the lot of you," said Ra. He tore off his heavy, fur covered coat.

"No!" Di shouted, but it was too late, Ra dived, head first into the water.

Chapter 25

The others watched as Ra hit the water. He surfaced, already swimming hard. But, instead, of swimming for the shore, he flipped around and propelled himself around the iceberg and out into the open sea. Djo stared after him, disbelievingly.

"He's going for the boat," said Di, almost punching the air.

"He hasn't got a chance," said Djo. The little boat was bobbing about a third of the way between the iceberg and the whales, but Djo knew they could cover the distance in seconds. Ra was a strong swimmer, and his arms arced through the water, sending showers into the air which hit his arching back as he hauled himself, head down, through the water towards the boat.

"Come on," shouted Di. "You can do it!" The orcas were swimming in circles, leaping and playing. They hadn't spotted him yet, but their play was taking them closer and closer to the boat as Ra, on the other side swam frantically towards it.

The twins were cheering too now, following Di's lead. Djo hoped they would not have to see what he was sure was going to happen next. Djo turned and looked back at the shore. It was close. He could see how shallow the water was just a few paces from the iceberg.

A thought struck him, and he instantly hated himself for it. Ra had chosen to go for the boat - that had been his decision. Whether he'd just been showing off, or whether he really believed he could make it, it didn't matter now. The killer whales were bound to spot him before he made it. But that didn't mean they all had to die.

Maybe, just maybe, if the creatures did attack Ra, that would give the rest of them enough time to make it to the beach. Whatever Ra's motives, he had next to no chance of making it, and if the rest of them had the chance to survive...

Djo felt a sick, guilty feeling running through his stomach, but he knew that if the chance came, he would have to take it. Djo watched the whales. The moment they spotted Ra, he would have to act.

He tensed and watched them for what seemed like forever. When Di and the twins suddenly cheered, Djo snapped out of it. His eyes flicked back to the boat and it took him a second to realise that Ra had made it. He had been so focused on the whales, fearing every movement of their fins meant they were about to launch themselves into an attack, that he had not noticed Ra reaching the boat and flipping himself out of the water and into it.

Guilt flooded in, blotting out everything else in Djo's mind. He felt wretched and mean. Maybe Ra wasn't the selfish one after all. Maybe it was himself. He had let Leal be taken by the ice-bear instead of him. He had risked all of their lives on the boat, just to impress Di, and now he had been ready in an instant to sacrifice Ra for a chance at getting to the shore. Perhaps Ra had been right about him all the time.

Djo watched, cursing himself for his selfish thoughts, as Ra cautiously dipped an oar on one side, and then the other of the boat, silently edging it closer and closer to the iceberg. The orcas were still playing, just a little way away.

He let the boat drift a little, trying not to attract the attention of the whales, and quickly slipped it in around behind the iceberg where he could paddle it to the steep sloping sides of the ice, hidden from the orca's view.

"Come on, then!" Ra grinned up at them. Di was first, climbing down the side of the iceberg. She slid, half leaping, half falling towards the boat, and Ra caught her. They threw their arms around each other. Perhaps trying to steady themselves as the boat rocked. Perhaps in relief at being reunited. Djo felt a lonely jealous pang in his stomach. They let go, Di sitting at one end of the boat and Ra at the other, balancing it in the water. Djo guided Chi and Cha as they used the ice as a slide, skidding into the boat at the bottom.

Djo turned to slide down after them, and just as he let go of the top of the iceberg, he looked out over the sea. The ocean where the whales had been playing was now empty and calm. They were nowhere to be seen.

Djo slid down, scrabbling against the ice, and dropped right into the middle of the boat. It shook, and with the weight of all of them inside, it was low in the water. The bottom was damp, and it stank of mammoth, but it was still floating, and only a short row away was land and safety.

Ra shoved off from their iceberg, and they started to paddle for the shore. Djo looked back. Behind them it was a white, glistening mountain. It looked strange, grounded on this lush land, and yet at the same time, it had been their home for weeks. A small piece of their own world run aground on this strange, hot, green, tree-covered land. The sun sparkled from the ice on its peak, and Djo could see it melting. Water collected into rivers and poured from outcrops on its overhanging edges into the water.

Then he saw them in the water. Four fins, close together, speeding around the side of the iceberg towards them.

"Quick!" he shouted, and the children abandoned their attempts at paddling quietly. They dug their bone oars deep into the water and threw up huge arcs of spray as they splashed frantically towards the land.

Djo's oar struck sand under the boat. They were nearly there. He braced against it and pushed the boat on like a punt. Behind them, the orcas were almost in striking distance. In shallow water, their whole, huge shapes were visible.

Another stroke with the oars and they were in knee deep water. The bottom of the boat was scraping on the sand.

"Come on!" shouted Ra, leaping out of the boat with one of the twins under each arm. He floundered towards the shore. Djo followed with Di right behind him. They struggled through the water. Behind them, Djo could see huge shapes rearing out of the water.

Di stumbled, falling over. One of the orcas was heading right towards her. Djo reached out and grabbed her arm, hauling her out of the way as a huge pair of jaws powered past, leaving one of the orcas stranded, flapping on the sand, its huge tail slapping the water behind them as it fought to turn itself back around.

Djo half ran, half dragged himself out of the water, and up the beach, still holding Di, who collapsed onto the sand beside him. A little further up, Ra, Cha and Chi were dripping and gasping on the shore.

The children watched as the beached whale turned its huge body and flapped out to sea. Meanwhile, its companions were setting to work on the boat, tearing it apart in their frustrated rage. The last remains of the old woolly mammoth guts were burst and shredded until all that was left was a few shreds of hairless skin, and bones, washed up on the shore.

The children looked at them.

"No way back now," Ra said. Di burst into tears.

Chapter 26

They sat, exhausted in the sand for a long time, watching the whales smash the boat apart, and then eventually give up and leave, their fins disappearing into the distance past the stranded iceberg. It was hot, and they slowly dried.

Djo looked over to Ra who was cradling Di in his arms while she sobbed. Eventually, she noticed a cut on Ra's leg, and busied herself cleaning it out while Ra pretended it didn't hurt. The twins were playing around the couple.

Djo watched them. Ra had saved them, but Djo couldn't help being angry at him anyway. He couldn't decide why. It was something to do with the way Di seemed so eager to deal with his stupid wound. Either that or it was the way he sat, his chest bare in the sun, his face stuck out like he didn't care about anything. Preening like a famous hunter.

It wasn't really Ra who had saved them, thought Djo suddenly. Ra had swum for the boat - but that had been a dumb risk. He'd been lucky to live. It was Djo whose idea it had been to build a boat. Djo whose design stayed afloat even when the iceberg tipped. Djo's boat that had brought them to the shore. Djo was the real hero.

But nobody remembered that, of course. By which he meant Di didn't remember. Because Di was the one that really mattered. Sitting on this strange beach, far from home, he could see it now. Di was what everything had always been about. She was the reason for every decision, every choice he ever made.

And as he looked across at the two of them together, he saw just as clearly that something had changed. She couldn't possibly have known what he was thinking, as Ra swam for the boat, and yet, somehow, that moment had changed the group. Before, they had been five children marooned and trying to survive. Now they were two groups. Djo and the twins were one, and Di and Ra were the other.

Djo pushed the thought from his head. Whatever happened, they had to survive, and sitting on the beach all day wasn't a good plan. He stood up, looking into the forest.

"We have to find out where we are," said Djo. Di and Ra looked up, and followed Djo's gaze up the beach and into the thick forest. It looked dark in there.

"I know where we are," said Cha. She was tugging at Di's arm.

"We're lost. That's all that matters," said Di.

"No we're not. I know where we are," said Cha.

"She's right," said Ra. "Doesn't matter where we are. We're here."

"No! We need to think this through," said Djo.

"We've had enough of your thinking!" spat Ra, "We need food, that's all. You can build a fire while I go and hunt it for you." Djo scowled at him. Thinking your way out of a problem just didn't compare to swimming a few strokes to somebody else's boat. Ra was the big hero now. But he was really milking it with this great leader, great hunter act. Ra must be just as scared and just as tired as the rest of them. Why couldn't he admit it?

"But I know where we are," said Cha.

"Ok," said Di, smiling down at the child. "Where are we?"

"We're in the Land of Monsters," said Cha.

Djo knelt down beside the little boy. The twins must be more scared than any of them, he thought. "Listen," he said, "all that was just campfire stories. They're just there to stop people trying to cross the ice. There isn't really a Land of Monsters." He held Cha's shoulders. "They're just funny stories. You don't need to worry."

"What's that, then?" said Cha. He pointed back down the beach behind Djo.

The children followed Cha's gaze, and what they saw, lazily chewing the leaves from the top of the trees was, quite definitely, a monster.

Chapter 27

Standing on its thick hind legs, it was taller than a mammoth, and covered in shiny brown fur. Huge arms, ending in giant hooked claws, reached out in front of it, scooping down branches towards its face. A pink tongue, which must have been as long and as thick as an adult's arm, snaked out of the mouth, pulling in leaves. The strange creature turned slowly to look at them. It let go of the branch, which sprang back up with huge force, and it shuffled lazily around to face the children, tilting its head on one side as if trying to work out what they were.

Ra acted immediately. He grabbed Djo's spear out of his belt hand and put himself in front of the group. He raised it high, ready to confront the huge beast. The creature was three times his height, and the huge clawed arms swung slowly in front of it as it watched Ra advancing with the relaxed disinterest of a beast which knew it could break him with a single swing of its great arm.

"Stop!" shouted Djo.

Ra kept advancing. "We have to kill it before it kills us!" he whispered over his shoulder.

"No!" Djo ran up to him, and put his hand on the spear, pushing it down into the sand. "We have to think about this!"

"What are you talking about?" said Ra.

"Look at it," said Djo. "We don't know what it is or what it can do. But we do know It's a plant eater!"

"So?"

"So look at those claws - if you attack it you'll get us all killed," said Djo. About fifty paces up the beach, the creature crouched down onto all fours, and started to advance slowly towards them. Ra looked at its huge bulk, and swallowed hard.

"What do you think we should do then, maker boy?"

"I think we should all just back up slowly," said Djo carefully. He began to do so, and Di, and the twins followed. Ra hesitated, but the beast was getting closer, and eventually, he started retreating. "Now, I think we should go into the trees," said Djo, without taking his eyes off the claws crunching slowly across the sand towards them, "It won't be able to follow us there so easily." They moved back further, between the closely packed trees. On the sand, they watched as the creature walked right up to the biggest tree, hauled itself onto its hind legs, and calmly started feeding again. Its body blocked out the light.

"What now?" said Di. Djo grabbed his spear back out of Ra's hand. Ra glared at him and snatched it back instantly.

"I'll take that," he said.

"It's my spear!" said Djo.

"Which you don't know how to use," said Ra. "I lost mine saving your life, in case you'd forgotten." Ra shoved the spear into his own belt. "So I guess you owe it to me."

"Let him have it," said Di to Djo. "We don't know what else is out here." Djo felt like she had slapped him. He was about to argue when she added, "What do you think we should do now?" Djo looked around.

"We need to find water, then shelter, then fire, then food." he said. "We should get to high ground first so we can find out where we are."

Ra grunted, but followed into the forest.

Djo led the group, picking his way between the close packed trees. This was a strange world. Oppressively hot, the jungle steamed, and their mammoth fur clothes were heavy and thick. In the trees were birds Djo didn't recognise, and disconcerting sounds came from all around - calls, growls, and distant crashes. One thing was for sure - they were not alone in this forest. Even if Di was right about the spear, Djo felt very vulnerable without a weapon.

Still, he kept quiet, avoided the nervous looks of the others, and led the group gradually uphill.

Chapter 28

The ground rose more and more steeply. There were rocks amongst the leaves, and soon there were boulders too. After a few minutes more, the group scrambled over them, up and up. Djo could feel the sweat running down his back under his thick coat. Ra had pushed his way to the front of the group, by now and every few feet, he stopped them, looking down at the ground, and poking at broken twigs. At one point, there was a big pile of dung across their path, and Ra made a big show of crouching, rolling it between his fingers, sniffing it, and shaking his head. Djo sighed. He was really showing off now.

"Come on!" said Djo. "We all know you're a great hunter - but we need water and shelter first!" Ra swung round. He drew himself up, right in front of Djo, glaring down at him. Djo's face was level with his chest.

"There's something here," said Ra, "in this forest." .

Djo shrugged. "What?" he said.

"I don't know," said Ra, "but it's big."

"The thing at the beach?" said Di.

Ra shook his head. "These tracks are like nothing I've ever seen. Not a mammoth, not an ice-bear - but..."

"But what?" said Djo.

Ra pointed at the dung. "Whatever left that eats meat. Lots of it."

"You're scaring the twins," said Djo.

"We should all be scared," said Ra, darkly.

"Well, the higher we get the harder we are to follow," said Djo.

Ra didn't look convinced, but he followed as Djo scrambled uphill.

As suddenly as it had begun, the forest ended. Forced to walk sideways along the mountain by the increasingly huge boulders in their way, Djo and the rest of the children found themselves suddenly walking out on a huge, flat topped rock which jutted out high above the ground. Behind this platform, the mountain rose, its thick trees giving way to scrubby bushes and eventually bare rock.

In front, the mountain dropped steeply away. The rock itself formed an overhanging cliff high enough to clear the tops of the trees in front. standing on it, Djo could see over the mountain they had climbed and out to the far horizon.

From where he stood he could suddenly see everything. Mountains in the distance were a rocky blue, speckled and capped with brilliant white. Closer, and down below them, he could see the lush, green forest break suddenly at a thin, silver river into open plains stretching for what looked like a dozen days' walk into the distance. Tall grass, short grass, sun-baked earth. Here and there, patches of trees sprouted in the open wilderness like hunting parties sent out from the forest to forage on the plain.

The landscape awed him. It was more varied and more beautiful than anything he had ever seen. Next to the frozen scrubland of home, and the terrifying emptiness of the ancient ice that formed The Great Barrier, this was a landscape beyond imagination. As he stared, as it slowly dawned on him what the brown specks dotted over the landscape really meant, Djo was frozen to the spot, the air squeezed from his body like a hand pressed on his chest.

Animals.

Thousands of them. Their strange details lost in the distance of the plains, their shapes varied and bizarre. Impossible numbers of the strangest monsters Djo had ever imagined teemed across the land, an unending stream of fur and muscle, teeth and claws.

The stories had been right. This was indeed the land of monsters.

Much would have been unfamiliar to the young explorers in these new lands of what we now call North America. As far as we know, no humans had ever set foot there.

The landscape would have been strange enough, but the animals would have been completely unknown. The animal they have just met, the Eremotherium, is a giant relative of the sloth, weighing around three tonnes, and was one of the largest land mammals ever to have existed. It was very well armed with its huge claws, but it was a herbivore and used them mainly to hook down the branches of the trees on which it fed.

However, Eremotherium was not the only resident of the new land, and many of the other creatures were not nearly so friendly.

When the first humans arrived in America, the plains were teeming with huge creatures. There were many strange species of elephant, huge camels and massive herds of buffalo. But it got stranger: as well as the giant ground sloths there were armadillos the size of cars, tapirs, sabre-toothed cats, and dire wolves (one and a half times as big as the wolves of today). And there was another predator too - one much more fearsome than anything mankind had ever faced before...

Chapter 29

The children stood for a long time, looking out over the new land. Djo's mind was reeling. Were there only monsters here? Was everything deadly? He looked at the twins playing beside him. How could he hope to protect them here? This place was terrifying and he didn't even have his spear.

Beside him, Di and Ra were standing shoulder to shoulder grinning out at the new world as if it was their own private playground. How could they find anything to smile at in this mad place? Di looked over to Ra, her eyes sparkling. She reached out her hand and took Ra's.

"Our new home," she said.

Ra nodded.

Djo watched them, and suddenly he knew. It was time to be honest with himself. They belonged together, Di and Ra. They were so alike. He had always known it, even growing up. Everyone in the village had known it. The two hunters were always going to end up together. And from now on it was always going to be like this. Them together. Him looking after the children. Suddenly, Djo felt very alone.

"Plenty to hunt here," said Ra.

"Or plenty to hunt us," said Djo. He took the hands of the twins and led them away from the edge of the rock, leaving the other two to watch the sunset together, hand in hand.

He took the twins down underneath the rocky outcrop. The huge rock created an overhanging wall. It made, Djo thought, as good a place to make camp as they'd seen so far in this dangerous world. With the back of their camp a solid wall of rock, they would at least be protected on one side, but what else could they make a camp from?

Djo knew from the experience of his whole life that there was only one material from which a camp could be made: Mammoth. Nobody in the village had ever made a shelter with anything else. That first night on the hunt, they had slept in a muddy hole covered in spiky bushes, but they had at least had their mammoth furs as a cover against the cold.

Here, it was not cold. The warmth was one of the most alien things about this land, but neither, as far as Djo had seen, were there mammoths. There had not been a sign of one since they arrived. Mammoths had always been everything to Djo. The huge creatures provided the village with shelter, food, clothes, fuel for fires. They provided the bone for their weapons, and the inspiration for their stories. Mammoths were their gods and their demons. And now, perhaps there were none. Could humans even survive without mammoths? The idea seemed impossible to Djo.

He looked around. There were plenty of trees. Thick webs of branches spread out to block the light above them with needle-sharp leaves. Maybe, if they pulled down some branches, they could make some kind of roof.

The trees were tall and the thin, leafy branches were high up. Djo put a foot on the lowest and tried to haul himself up. He got about four steps before his foot slipped against the rough bark and he tumbled onto the forest floor. He tried again, pulling himself up, hugging the side of the tree, but it was hopeless. He was just too heavy to hold onto the trunk.

He tried a third time. This time, he got his leg onto the lowest branch and wriggled up until he was standing on it, but above him there was nothing to hold on to, nothing large enough to bear his weight, just thin, brittle nodules sticking out from the side of the tree. They would never hold him.

Suddenly, he heard a laugh from below him.

"Can I play?" said Chi, stepping up to the tree and grabbing the trunk.

"No, it's too dangerous," said Djo.

Chi, of course, took no notice. Laughing, she scooted straight up the side of the tree. In seconds, she was high above them. She held on with one hand, waving with the other.

"It's fun!" she said.

"Come down!" said Djo, but Chi was taking no notice, and now Cha too was scrambling up the next tree along, giggling mischievously to himself.

The twins waved at Djo from the upper branches.

He sighed. "Be careful, then," he said.

"It's easy," said Chi, demonstrating by hanging upside down on one leg from one of the top branches.

Djo winced. He needed to keep them hanging onto the tree. Showing off like that could get them killed. "Can you break off some of the little branches?" he said, "I want them for a camp."

The twins responded immediately, and soon little branches and leaves were raining down around Djo. They were spiky but spread out in flat mats. He gathered them up and started to arrange them against the wall of rock. The larger ones, he used as struts to form a triangular camp. The smaller sticks, he wove between the large branches into tight sheets, and, from there, he worked quickly, weaving the individual twigs between them. Soon, the camp was beginning to take shape. It was a strange, dark green thatch, but in the forest, it would at least be shelter, and camouflage from whatever hunted there.

When the twins got tired of their game at the top of the trees, they clambered down as easily as they had climbed up, and started to help him push leaves from shrubs into the gaps in the shelter.

Djo tried to focus on the work, but all the time, from the top of the rock, above him, he could hear Ra and Di talking. Pointing out animals, on the plain below, and trying to work out how to kill them. He forced himself to block out the sound of their happy voices, and the terrible feeling that was crawling into his chest. Every laugh from above felt like a black tendril, creeping between his ribs and wrapping itself around his heart, crushing the life from it.

He tried to concentrate on weaving the branches together, but sadness was a weight, pulling him down, and blurring his eyes with tears. He forced the feeling back, telling himself he was stupid to even allow these thoughts to enter his head. And as he did so, jealousy replaced sadness, crawling up through him to strangle his throat. Ra was strong, brave, Ra did not waste time thinking. He just acted. Ra would not have stood, frozen in the snow while the ice-bear dragged Leal away.

As Djo was being torn apart, he told himself his feelings didn't matter. What mattered was the twins, and their survival depended on the shelter as much as it depended on Ra and Di, and what they could hunt. He crushed his jealousy down into a tiny, seed and forced it away into his stomach. And as he did so, another feeling started to grow out of it. Anger.

Djo had shown them how to make the camp. How to make the boat. He deserved some respect for that. What right did Ra have to bully him constantly? To threaten him. To insult him. To take his spear? Without Djo, Di wouldn't even be here. She would have vanished on that first night beside the glacier. She would probably be dead by now, in the snow. Without Djo, they would all be dead.

Even now, while they were holding hands and giggling on top of the rock, Djo was building a shelter for them.

Eventually, when Djo stood back, the anger still growing inside him, the camp looked sort of finished. He had never slept in, never even seen, a camp like it. The idea of sleeping under leaves seemed mad, but, he thought, there was no reason why it couldn't work. Anyway, without help from the other two, it was the best he could do.

Chapter 30

"What is this rubbish?" Ra laughed as the couple finally came down from the top of the rock.

Djo spun around. They were standing together. Their shoulders touching. Ra was grinning.

"It's our camp!" said Chi, "we made it!"

"It looks like you made it!" said Ra, poking at the leafy mess of the roof. "Where's the real one?"

Djo bit his lip as he saw Di trying not to snigger behind Ra. "This is all we've got," said Djo quietly.

"I'm not sleeping in this," said Ra.

Djo clenched his fists. He felt his face burning red.

"Well, get me ten mammoths and I'll build you one just like home," he said. "In the meantime, this is the best I can do."

And in that moment, Djo felt the anger spread inside him like a heat that filled him from his feet to his fists and up through his spine to flood his brain. Djo hated Ra. He hated him more than he had ever hated anyone in his life. He stepped up to stare Ra directly in his stupid, grinning face.

"I ought to kick you back down to the beach," said Ra, closing his hands into fists.

Suddenly, it was happening. Djo wasn't sure who threw the first punch, but the two boys were locked in an ugly kicking, gouging, ball. Djo felt his fist connect with Ra's face. Felt Ra's knee in his stomach. Felt the crack of branches beneath them as they crashed into the shelter. Djo wheeled his arms and legs in frantic fury. He wasn't thinking, just tearing and pounding at Ra.

By now he could hear Di shouting. The twins screaming. But none of it mattered. Only his hatred for Ra. He felt the wall of rock, and twisted around to slam Ra's back into it. He felt Ra's fist collide with his nose. Djo's fingers gripped his hair, and he yanked. Then the two were rolling over and over down the hill until they both smashed heavily into the trunk of a tree, and split apart.

When he staggered to his feet, Ra was running at him. In his hand, his spear, fist close to the blade as though it was a cutting knife. Djo saw that look of mad fury in his eyes again. Djo tensed. If this was to the death then so be it.

He grabbed Ra's arm, and smashed a shoulder into his chest. They grappled, faces pressed together. Djo could see the blade in Ra's hand pressing closer and closer to his neck as he struggled against the older boy's much stronger grip.

Djo wriggled his other hand and managed to get it up between them to his neck where his Firstblade was hanging on its cord. His fingers grasped it and desperately yanked. In one movement, the blade came free, and Djo felt it meet the flesh of Ra's cheek, scraping across. The older boy sprang back, clutching his face. Blood seeped between his fingers. He pulled his hand away and looked, disbelievingly at it. A deep cut had opened up from his ear to the side of his nose. It was pouring blood.

Suddenly, Di was standing between them, holding the two apart. "Stop!" she was yelling.

Djo didn't care. He pushed forward against her hand. She stood firm and glared at Djo, then back at Ra.

"Stop!" she said again.

The two boys didn't move. They stood, breathing heavily, blades in their fists.

After a while, she spoke slowly and quietly to Djo. "We're going to go now," she said. "We need food."

Ra didn't move for a few seconds. He and Djo stared at each other.

"Come on," she said to Ra, putting her hand on his arm, "let's go."

Ra finally broke eye contact with Djo, and turned to her.

"Come on," he said. "He's only slowing us down."

As the couple strode off into the woods, Di flashed a last look back at Djo. He wasn't sure if it was a warning, or an apology, or a goodbye. It didn't matter, he supposed, because in a second, the two of them had vanished down the mountainside.

Chapter 31

Djo was left, standing, his breath coming in short bursts, as the anger slowly faded. He opened his hand and looked down at his Firstblade. Ra's blood was on it. His hand was shaking as the feelings of fear and anger subsided.

When he looked up again, the twins were both staring at him, silently, confused horror on their faces. Whatever had held the group together through the long days on the iceberg, had suddenly broken on the top of that rock. Djo realised the twins could not understand why, and he could not explain it to them.

"Where have they gone?" said Chi.

"I don't know," said Djo.

"Have they gone hunting?"

"I don't know," he said again. But he did know. Ra would leave them in a heartbeat if he thought he had a better chance without them. And that look Di had given him. She had made her choice.

"When will they be back?" said Cha. "I'm hungry."

Djo looked at the ground. They wouldn't be back, ever. But how could he tell the children that?

"We need to build a fire," he said, quickly. He placed his Firstblade back around his neck, and forced all thoughts from his mind. The only thing that mattered now was survival, and survival meant fire. Fire, shelter, water, food. They had shelter, or sorts, and, of the other three, fire was the one problem he felt he could solve.

Even that wasn't going to be easy. If he had a handful of mammoth hair, and some belly fat then, even in a cold wind and on frozen ground, he could have had a rising flame in no time. But here he would have to discover a whole new way of doing it.

He could still make a spark, he thought. The bow and spindle he carried in his belt would work fine. He could spin them together until they smoked and glowed red, but with no fur, what could he use to turn that glow into flame?

He looked around him. The ground was carpeted in dry leaves. Perhaps they would burn. He gathered a pile together and held them in his hands in a ball as if they were mammoth hair. They felt odd and wrong, but when he made a smoking ember, placed it at the centre of the ball, and blew into it, the ball caught almost immediately.

He placed it onto the ground, and started to pile small sticks around it. They caught too. This was easier than he had thought and for the first time he began to feel a little better. As the twins watched, he placed a larger branch across the fire. It spat and crackled, but soon started to smoke and glow red.

He started to bring bigger and bigger branches to the fire, creating a towering pyramid of flame. Soon, it was nearly as tall as him. It created a wall of heat all around it, and Djo had to stand away and throw more branches onto it from a distance. This was nothing like the tiny, meagre fires they lit back at home, where everything was wet and every flammable object was a precious resource. This was the biggest fire Djo had ever seen in his life. The flames leapt high into the sky, and billows of smoke poured upwards.

The twins were laughing by now, the fight forgotten as they danced around the towering flames. Even Djo allowed himself a little smile. Ra and Di were out there somewhere, hunting together, but neither of them were as good at fire making as he was. Whatever they caught they'd have to eat it raw. It would serve them right thought Djo as he watched the twins playing.

Djo barely even noticed the base of the fire spreading slowly outwards towards the camp. Every fire he had ever lit had been on snow, or ice cold, wet ground. He had never given a moment's thought to what might happen if everything around his fire could be burnt, if even the ground itself were covered in dry, dead leaves. That idea had simply never been a part of Djo's world. He watched the flames in wonder as they grew and grew, and he, and the twins stepped further and further away from it.

Chapter 32

Without warning, the wind changed direction. The flame leaned over, and licked a nearby tree. In seconds, it was fully alight. The flames raced up the rough bark, and the leafy canopy ignited as though it were soaked in fat. The main fire itself spat and crackled, and one of the logs shifted. The pile of branches collapsed, and the fire tumbled into pieces, sending hot logs rolling into Djo's carefully built camp. Djo dived towards it, trying to kick the branches away, but he was forced back by the heat. All he could do was watch as the little shelter blazed.

There was a creak from behind him, and Djo span around just in time to see a branch crash from a flaming tree, setting the ground around it on fire. He looked up. The tree itself shook, and a great cracking, tearing sound came from its trunk. Djo looked up. It was falling towards them.

Djo grabbed Chi and Cha and hurled them back against the wall of rock behind them, diving back under the rock himself just in time for the massive trunk to smash into the boulder above them. It held, leaning diagonally against the wall of rock, the blackened trunk, still smouldering. The leafy top of the tree, now completely consumed in flames, was pinned against the boulder. Those burning branches were the only thing now stopping the trunk from crashing down on top of them.

They would have to make a run before it snapped and fell on top of them, but, through the smoke, Djo could see that the whole forest was burning around them. How could that happen so fast?

Chi and Cha were staring at him, faces filthy with soot, eyes wide with fear. He thought fast. They couldn't stay here. The tree was creaking and cracking. It could come down on them at any second, and the smoke was getting thicker and thicker. But where could they run to? Where was safe? He grabbed the twins' hands.

"Come on," he shouted. He took a gulp of air, and held his breath, launching himself forward through the stinging hot branches, and out.

The smoke was so thick, he could barely see where he was going, but to his left, the wall of rock was just visible as a huge, dark shadow. He pulled them close to it, and led them uphill, following the shape of the massive boulder.

The fire was spreading fast, now, and there was smoke and flame all around them, but Djo dragged the twins on up around the side of the rock.

Djo's throat was burning, and he could barely stand the heat, but finally they reached the stone plateau. He forced them forward towards the cliff edge, and they broke through into clear, smokeless air. Behind them, the forest was on fire, but at least the rock they were standing on couldn't burn, and it jutted just far enough out over the side of the mountain to be clear of the billowing smoke. Out on the rocky outcrop, Djo and the twins stood, gasping and choking.

Chapter 33

It didn't get dark that night. It got yellow. As the fire spread down through the forest, it grew huge and wild, roaring like a raging monster. A huge ring of dark smoke spread out from the top of the mountain. It curved out above them, huge and threatening like the landscape of a nightmare. The sky felt ready to fall down and crush them under its smoky mountains. The glow of the flame raging across the mountainside reflected off the cloud, bathing everything in a deep, unhealthy orange light.

Djo and the twins huddled at the edge of the rock. On one side of them, a sheer drop into the smoking forest, and down beyond that to the plain, now shrouded in shadow. On the other, a wall of heat and smoke. As it shifted, the ghosts of trees faded into and out of sight, silhouetted against the glow of their burning neighbours.

It was only the wind that saved them. The hot, dry wind that blew up the side of the mountain, sucked by the heat of the flames, dragging their smoke into the sky. The wind, hauled up from the plain fanned the flames, but at the same time pushed them back against the mountainside. It was only this wind, sculpting around the shape of the jutting rock that created a tiny, safe island of air in the ocean of smoke around them.

The air was not fresh. It stank of burning, and was heavy with floating white and glowing orange fragments. It was breathable, but Djo knew, if the wind shifted, they would be dead in minutes.

He held the twins close to him, and waited. Chi and Cha fell almost instantly asleep in his arms. He thought back. He hadn't slept since he was jolted awake by the iceberg cracking in half. That seemed so long ago now. He had been running on excitement ever since.

His head began to nod. He fought it but exhaustion was catching up with him. Before he knew what was happening, he felt a breeze against his face. His eyes flicked open and he was instantly blinded by smoke.

The wind had turned! He gasped. The air was thick and choking. He staggered to his feet. He coughed, and gulped another lung full of suffocating smoke. He looked around. There was nowhere to go. He felt dizzy, his head spinning, his eyes stinging.

Beside him the twins lay on the hard stone. He reached down, and then drew his hand back. As the blackness overtook his mind, there was time for just one thought: "Don't wake them. If they have to die, let it be in their sleep."

He felt his legs weaken and wobble. There was a sickening jolt as he fell to his knees on the rock, and pitched sideways, choking. The blackness crawled across his consciousness, and then he felt nothing.

Chapter 34

When Djo awoke, he was soaked. Rain was pouring from a dark morning sky, and the air smelled of damp, burned wood. Rotten and black. His head was throbbing. He forced his eyes slowly open. They were sore and sticky. He raised his head. The twins were lying motionless a few paces away.

Djo scrambled to his knees and crawled over to them. He grabbed Chi by the shoulder, and pulled her over onto her back. Her face was a white mask, stained with a dusting of black where the ash had settled on her in the night. She didn't seem to be breathing. Djo grabbed the fur wrapped around her shoulders and shook her hard. Her head flopped forward and then limply fell back.

He stared at her for a moment, and then suddenly, she coughed into life. She opened her eyes and started to cry. Beside her, her brother, sat up. Djo held out his arms and grasped the twins, hugging them so tightly they squirmed in his grip. He almost burst into tears himself.

"I'm sorry," he said, over and over again. "I'm so sorry!"

Eventually he let go, and stumbled to the edge of the rock to look out over the mountainside. The full impact of what he had done hit him like a wall of ice.

The forest was a dark, smouldering graveyard of black, broken trees. From the rock where he had started the fire, right down to the sea on one side, and the plains on the other, the ground was an ashen mess of white and black dust and rain soaked mush. There were fallen trees consumed entirely by fire. Others were black sticks, stripped of branches and leaves. Here and there, smoke was still rising, but mostly the fire had burnt itself out or been quenched by the rains.

What had been the lushest, most alive place Djo had ever seen in his life was now a lonely, desolate, stinking wasteland. It was as lifeless as the glacier they had left so long ago, only it was worse, because this place had been so green. So beautiful. And its destruction had been completely and utterly his fault.

Somewhere out there, were Di and Ra. His stupidity had almost certainly killed them. He pictured them lying side by side. Maybe the fire had raced down the hill faster than they could run. Maybe they hadn't seen it until it was too late, and they had found themselves cut off, surrounded by a ring of fire. Maybe they had huddled together as it had closed in and finally consumed them.

Or - perhaps they had escaped. Djo looked down the hill to the plain below. If they were going to hunt, they might have gone there. But surely it was too far. Even if they had been running. Even if they had taken the straightest route. They would almost certainly not have made it.

A horrid, sick, part of him hoped they hadn't. It would serve them right. He looked back at the twins. Walking out on Djo was one thing. There was no place for him in their stupid lovey-dovey game, and that was fine. If that was what they wanted. But abandoning the twins was something else. She knew - both of them knew - that Djo couldn't look after them on his own. They might as well have stabbed the twins to death with their spears.

With Djo's spear.

For the first time, it occurred to Djo that when they left, Ra had taken Djo's spear. He had left them with nothing to defend themselves with. Nothing to hunt with, if he even knew how to hunt. What was more, he couldn't make another, not without mammoth bone, and without a spear...

"I'm thirsty," said Cha suddenly.

"Me too," said Chi, "and I'm hungry."

Of course they were. Djo realised his own throat was dry and sore, and his belly was empty. They would have to find food and water soon. With a sickening feeling, Djo realised he knew where to find it.

Chapter 35

He had spotted it when they first arrived at the outcrop. Down at the bottom of the mountain, where the forest met the plain, a thin line glistened in the morning sun, silver against the black lines of burned trees. A river.

He knew they had to go there. He had known from the moment he saw it. Nothing could live without fresh water for long, but that was the problem. It was rule one of the hunt. Everything had to drink. Every creature from the smallest mouse to the greatest mammoth. And from where he stood, Djo could see that the river was the only water for miles around. If this really was the land of monsters, then that tiny stream of silver would be the one place where he could be utterly sure all the monsters had to come.

And now, Djo had to go there too. He had to go now. And he had to take the little twins with him. He didn't even have a weapon.

Except, of course, that he did. And now, with nothing else left, it was time to use it.

Djo's fingers found the totem strung around his neck. His Firstblade. The one he had carved with his father. It seemed so long ago. He pulled it over his head and examined it.

He knew the rules. The Firstblade was a marker, not a weapon. It existed only to tell you who you were. Where you had come from. How far you had grown. With each new blade you struck, your skills would advance. Your maturity would grow. And each time you compared your Firstblade to your last, you measured yourself. Your journey. You connected to your younger self and remained true to your own spirit.

The shape of the blade was his history. The history of his village. Every barb in its traditional point meant something. An imprint that went back through the generations. The mark of every hunter who had compared his blade to those who taught him, stretching back through time.

Djo remembered how his Firstblade had been ridiculed by Ra. How his father had taken it to show the elders, and then handed it back, stern-faced without a word. It must be a poor blade, and no wonder. What he had thought of while he carved it was Leal, his poor sister, taken by an ice-bear while he watched and did nothing. He felt the edge. Sharp. The guilt of Leal's memory in every chip of its carving. The guilt of Ra's blood dried on its surface, and now the guilt of this fire would be seared into its use.

And while he had carried it around his neck, he had done nothing to redeem it. The blades he had fashioned on the iceberg were hasty, rough things, for cutting and sewing. Chipped, without the right tools, from fresh, unseasoned bone. They were even worse. And now, with no other weapons, and no bones to fashion more, abandoned in the Land of Monsters, Djo's Firstblade, his only connection with his people, was all he had. As he split a charred stick, and wedged the blade into it to form a spear, winding its twine over and over itself to form a tight binding, it felt like his final step backwards.

Forest fires are an important part of the natural cycles. The great destruction they cause clears the way for new trees and plants to flourish. However, it also disrupts the wildlife of the forest. Territories fought for and won over years are suddenly wiped out, and the whole violent battle of ownership has to begin again for every creature.

The balance of predators and prey shifts, and the creatures who live there are forced to find new territories and new sources of food.

After the fire, the surviving predators of the forest would become unpredictable and dangerous, finding themselves in a whole new environment. The predators of the plain too would suddenly discover they could move through the more open forest in search of a meal...

Chapter 36

They had taken the long way down. The dead, burned-out wood was an eerie place. The black smoke cloud was slowly vanishing, but above it, the heavy, grey rain clouds were still thick and dark. The forest was horribly quiet. The birds were gone. The rustling leaves were burnt to ash. Nothing searched for food in the undergrowth. The whining, rasping sounds of the insects were cut off. The only noise was the hiss of damp, hot ash, steaming. The forest smelled stale and dead. Here and there, the charred bones of forest creatures lay. Those that had not fled had been overtaken by fire and smoke, and now lay, unrecognisable in the ruins of their home. When everything cooled, the scavengers would come, but for now, the black corpses lay where they had fallen.

Djo stumbled through the desolation, guilt pressing heavily on his back, the twins trailing behind, complaining of their thirst. He wondered what the elders would have said. He had killed all these animals. Was he now responsible for the anger of their spirits? If so, he would have to bury a lot of blades. And, if the angry spirits wandered the Land of Monsters forever, then what happened to animals who died here? What would the elders say to that?

It didn't matter. He was beyond all that now. The elders couldn't help him here. They had never gone beyond the ice. They had never crossed the ocean. They had never set foot in this strange hot, green land. They knew nothing. He walked on.

Where the rain had made it to the ground, it had turned the ash to a filthy mud which clung to their boots. Where it had not, each step threw up clouds of fine, choking white dust.

Djo pressed on ahead of the twins, wanting to be on his own as they slowly trudged downhill through the desolation, towards the river. Suddenly, he froze.

"Shh!" he hissed.

The twins stood still behind him. He motioned for them to follow close. Up ahead, Djo could hear the sound of running water.

Keeping low, he crept to the edge of the trees. He peered through between the trunks. A few paces away, the ground sloped down into the clear river.

As soon as he saw the water, Djo's throat started to burn. His mouth felt unbearably dry. He'd been forcing himself to think only of getting the twins through the forest, but now that he saw the water, he became aware of how badly he needed to drink. The last water he had tasted was a handful of snow, gouged from the iceberg just before it ran aground. Now, his mind was screaming at him to run down to the river and scoop up huge handfuls of cold, clear water.

But, no. However tempting it was, all he could see between the trees was a tiny section of the river. A few paces in either direction there could be anything waiting. As they had climbed up to the plateau the previous day, Ra had been convinced there was something in the forest. Something huge that ate meat. What if it were here waiting for them?

Slightly to his left, a patch of churned mud had preserved a single green bush close to the river's edge. Even from where he was standing, he could see a confused mess of huge, strange footprints in the churned mud. Something had been here, and recently. More likely, several somethings. Several different kinds of huge beasts had been to the river, and for all Djo knew, they were still here, just out of sight.

But the bush itself offered hope. If they could just make it there, they could get under cover, and they would have a chance of slipping down to the water's edge without being seen by whatever else was drinking.

Looking at the ground between the trees and the bush, he counted the steps. Planned his strides. He told the twins to wait until he was safely in the bushes so that he could asses the danger, then he crouched, like a runner, ready for the sprint across open ground. He held his breath, focused on the bush. This was the most dangerous moment.

Chapter 37

Suddenly from behind them, there was the sound of splitting wood. Djo spun around. It was the monster from the beach. Huge, disorientated in the unfamiliar landscape of the burnt forest, it was charging towards the river, and they were directly in its path.

The monster was running, its two back legs striding, staggering over the ground, throwing up clouds of ash. Its huge arms were curled into fists, the long claws sticking upward as it scraped the ground in front of it to keep its body from toppling forward. Djo could tell the creature had suffered in the fire. Its fur was singed and matted, its back coated with a layer of white ash. A huge red, black smear of melted hair and charred flesh was carved into its side.

"Run," Djo shouted, grabbing the twins and forcing them out from the cover of the trees and down towards the water.

Their fur boots slipped and skidded on the wet pebbles of the beach, throwing up rattling arcs of stones around them.

The beast came after. It wasn't heading for them, just for the water, but it swung its huge claws in front of it as it ran. Each sweep could have thrown the three of them twenty paces. Each claw could have torn a deep gash through clothes, skin and internal organs.

Djo pulled the twins to one side, hurling all of them along the riverbank without even looking where they were going. The beast ignored them completely, stopped, looked back into the trees for a moment, and then crashed down onto all fours, sticking its head deep into the water to drink.

Djo spun around. The three of them were exposed now, trapped in the open between the burned wood, the drinking monster and the deep, fast flowing river. His eyes scanned for cover. At the river's edge, three huge round boulders were clustered. He yanked the children towards them, but they had only taken two steps when one of the boulders moved.

Djo skidded to a stop, staring in disbelief. The boulder shook, and started to laboriously wobble around in a circle. It was a rounded dome, as tall as he was, and maybe ten paces around. Earth-brown. Now that he was closer, he could see it was not stone. It was made of something between tusk and leather, a hard rough surface with a few coarse hairs sprouting from it. A short tail curled out from underneath behind it. At the other end, now facing him, another, smaller boulder rose from the water. A head. Square and armoured with heavy, scaly plates. It opened its mouth, and bellowed, a pink, blunt-toothed mouth, tiny compared to the massive bulb of the body, or shell, or whatever it was. It roared its angry challenge at them.

Djo readied his spear. His Firstblade glinted sharp at the end of it. He looked for a weak spot. The creature's armour covered it with not the slightest gap. Why would a monster need such armour? What lived here that could threaten this rock of a creature?

The beast put its head down, threateningly, and crouched ready for a charge. Behind it, the two other rock monsters turned from the water and faced them. Djo pulled the twins behind him, but he knew that his own body would be no protection when this mountain of a creature charged them. It would crush the three of them into the stones, and barely notice.

He jabbed his spear as hard as he could, hoping to force the monster back. His blade scraped against the hard shell and glanced harmlessly off.

He struck again, aiming at the head. It was a clean shot, but the blade struck the thick scales, and the creature tossed its head angrily to the side, forcing the spear away. It left not a scratch.

The creature was bearing down on them by now, swinging its head. Behind it, the other two were readying to charge.

Djo stood his ground, leveling the spear. Suddenly, a change came over the monsters. They froze, and then started to back away. Djo stepped forward. The lead animal turned and bolted down along the riverbank. For such a huge creature, it charged with amazing speed. The other two followed. Their massive bulks, swinging around and rocking improbably as they bounded, panicking away.

Djo straightened. He felt Chi tugging at his arm. There was something behind him. He turned, feeling its presence before he saw it. Feeling its shadow loom over him in the time it took him to turn his body to face it. Knowing it before he saw it. Something huge, strange, but oddly familiar. Djo turned, sensing that same old sweet sick smell. Wet grass and dry blood. He felt a cold, sick feeling deep in his stomach.

His old enemy was back.

The bear.

It had taken his sister, and now it had come for him.

But when he turned to face it, it was not what he had expected. This was the Land of Monsters. And this bear was a monster among monsters.

No pure white coat of perfect fur here. This was something else. Its coat was dark. Thick steaming mats of course clumped hair, smeared and soaked in mud and blood, and ash. And it was huge. Twice the bulk of an ice bear. On all fours, it towered over Djo and the cowering children. But as he watched, it dipped its head, still staring at them, and reared up onto its back legs, stretching its great ash covered paws high into the sky, yellow claws like four huge blades in each black, padded hand. It was taller now than a mammoth. It took one step towards them, swaying on its muscled back legs, and its mouth fell open. The black lips peeled back to show gaping yellow fangs in a pink, almost human mouth so wide Djo felt it could have swallowed them whole. He saw the steam on its breath, the saliva on its fangs. The smell of its breath was overpowering now. A dank, rotten mix of sweat and meat, grass and hot anger.

It looked down, its eyes tiny black pits pin-pricked with white reflected light. They blazed with hot, demonic fury. And yet, that same old look that was burned into DJo's heart. That same calculating mind lurked behind the eyes. "Now," it seemed to say somewhere deep inside his mind, "now it is your turn." If the spirits of hunters' un-remembered kills really did stalk the earth, they were here in the eyes of this creature.

Djo could feel the panic rising in his stomach. His legs were weak. His brain was screaming, "Run!"

His father's words came back to him. After Leal had been taken, he had sat Djo down and told him what to do. "Stand your ground," he had said. "You cannot outrun a bear. He fears only fire."

But there was no fire here. Just Djo and the blade he had carved while thinking about his lost sister. Djo felt his spear in his hand, still raised high above his head. As the bear reared up in front of him, Djo summoned all his power. He leant back, pushing his back foot hard into the ground with his whole weight, tightening every muscle from his heel to his calf, his thigh, his stomach to his shoulder. felt his whole self focused on the tip of his spear. The very point of his Firstblade. This would have to be the throw of his life. He drove it forward, every muscle firing in sequence to propel the spear through the air and deep into the creature's body.

Djo felt it leave his hands, sure and powerful, and he watched as the blade spun and glinted, striking the bear in the centre of its chest.

Silence.

The bear froze. Looked down. Then with one arm, it smashed the spear from its body. The thin, sharpened bone of Djo's blade splintered and fell away in white pieces into the mud. There was no blood on it. It hadn't even penetrated the thick hair. The bear crashed onto all fours, its massive head staring down at Djo and the cowering twins. It roared in fury.

Djo closed his eyes.

Suddenly there was another roar from behind them. The creature from the beach had turned from its drinking, and seen the bear. Its path of escape blocked, it had reared up, ready to defend itself. The bear swung its black eyes from the little figure of Djo to the huge monster, and back, assessing the threat.

The panicking beach-monster swiped with its claws, and the bear ducked, rearing up and smashing the creature in the face with its own great paw. The monster staggered and then hurled its huge bulk at the bear.

Djo grabbed the twins, and dragged them from between the two giants, and plunged them, without thinking, into the river. Behind him, he could hear the smashing blows of the giants gouging and charging at each other. He hauled the twins out into the deeper part of the fast flowing river, and let the current take them, sweeping them downstream and away from the battle.

As the river carried them away, Djo could not tear his eyes from the battle on the bank. The bear was pulverising the monster. One huge claw after another, tore into it in blind fury. Fur and blood was flying into the air. The bear was tearing its prey apart. The poor monster's huge arms were trying to hold the bear off, but it just brushed them aside. Just before Djo and the twins were dragged out of sight, he saw the bear raise its bloodied head in victory, roaring its triumph into the sky before sinking its wide open mouth down onto the monster's neck to choke the last life from its victim.

The short-faced bear was the biggest predator of the American plains. Twice the size of a modern grizzly, and long-legged. Scientists have suggested it could have stood four metres high on two legs, and outrun a horse on four. It had long, reaching arms ending in massive 20cm claws and a stronger bite than any known land mammal.

The short-faced bear evolved amongst the mega-beasts of America: the dire wolves, the sabre toothed cats, the giant sloths, the huge hard-shelled glyptodon which Djo ran into at the water's edge. But even amongst these, it was a terrifying giant. The short-faced bear was possibly the most fearsome mammal land predator of all time. Since the dinosaurs, nothing like it has ever walked on land. To Djo, this must have been a creature straight out of his nightmares...

Chapter 38

The river finally widened and slowed enough for Djo and the twins to scramble, sputtering onto the flint pebbles of the bank.

After they had quenched the burning in their throats with the clear, cold water, they scooped from the shallows, Djo sat on the bank, breathing hard. His whole body was shaking with fear and exhaustion, his mind spinning. The monster bear was like nothing he had ever seen, and yet, he knew it was coming for him. It was his punishment. It was his fear, his failure, his hatred and jealousy. The guilt had been growing inside him since the ice-bear had taken Leal, and now that same spirit was returning to claim him.

Djo held out his arm. It was shaking. He struggled to control his breathing, to slow his heartbeat, and slowly his hand steadied. He looked around. At least they were safe for now. He could see a good distance all around. If anything was coming, they would at least get some warning. Up ahead, the river spilled out into the sea. On one side, the land flattened out into a wide field of scrubby grass. On the other, the burned poles of the dead forest petered out to the beach beyond them.

Cha was filled with the excitement of the escape. He jumped up and started to pretend he was the bear. He ran around, roaring and batting at plants with his paws. He would be just fine.

Chi was another matter. She sat, pale, wide-eyed, and staring at every crack of wood, every rattle of pebbles. Every sound of birds flying overhead made her gasp and start. She was shaking. Djo wanted to reassure her, but how could he? Her response to this terrifying land was the right one. It was Cha's joyous excitement that was misplaced.

Djo just sat next to her, and wished Di was with them.

He thought back to what had happened. His carefully carved Firstblade lay shattered in the mud. It hadn't even scratched the creature. Di or Ra might have done better, thrown harder. A better blade might have made a mark on the animal, but Djo knew one thing for sure. Even in the hands of the greatest hunter, the weapons of his people could not save them in this land.

If they wanted to survive here, they would need a new weapon. Something capable of bringing down a monster. And he had nothing. Not even a bone to carve one from, just a wrecked forest. Djo pictured himself facing the bear again. This time, armed with the only weapon he could find - a burnt stick.

Beside him, Chi started to scream. He spun around, eyes scanning the wood, the river, the scrubby bushes of the plain. What had she seen? Sabre-tooth? The bear? Something else?

He saw nothing.

"What is it?" he said.

She was crying uncontrollably now. She held up her fist. It was clenched tight. Blood was leaking through her fingers.

"Open your hand," said Djo.

She ignored him.

He grabbed her arm and prised her fingers open. A broken pebble fell from her hand.

"It's OK," said Djo. "It's just a cut. Let me look."

Chi's cries dropped to a sob. In her frozen fear, she had grabbed a stone and gripped it so hard that it had cut her. Djo scooped a handful of water, and washed the blood away. He couldn't blame her for her fear of this land. The poor child had been through enough to make an adult lose their mind. The fact that her brother showed no sign of being affected by it all was the surprising thing.

"It's OK," he said again. "See, not too bad."

The cut was a long one. A deep gash across her palm, but it would heal, if they lived long enough. He bound it in clean, wet leaves, tied around her hand with grass stems, and held her tight in his arms. Eventually, she began to calm.

Cha joined them, tucking his head under Djo's other arm, and snuggling into him, falling asleep instantly. Djo slowly rocked them. All they had was each other, now.

Chapter 39

"Be careful of the stones," Djo whispered. "Be careful of everything."

With his free hand, he picked up the pebble that had cut Chi. A drop of her blood still stained the round, brown white surface.

On one side, the pebble was pale and porous chalk. It was soft, worn round by time and the river. But where it had broken open, the inside was something else. Blue-black, and strangely transparent. On its surface, angled shards had broken away, leaving scoops and waves in the dark surface like a stormy sea, frozen in stone. It was beautiful in its hard, dangerous way, just like this land. Djo felt himself drawn to it. Where the chipped surface was freshly broken, he ran his thumb along the edge. It drew blood instantly. The edge was sharp. Sharper than a bone blade. Sharper than anything he had ever seen, and stronger too.

He stared at it. Back in the village, there were stone tools. Thin shards and arrow tips, but nothing like this. He needed something far bigger, stronger.

He turned the flint over and over in his hands and wondered. The stone was strong, but it had been broken. Freshly broken on this beach. And if it could be broken, that meant it could be worked. Formed. Shaped.

He carefully lowered the children to the ground, and left them sleeping, laying his coat over them. Chi shifted a little, and sobbed quietly, but she didn't wake up. He stood up and walked down to the water's edge. The riverside was scattered with stones. Some big, some small, some whole, round, pale pebbles. Some broken shards.

He selected two. One a long oval shape, pure white, and about the size of his hand. The other, a fist-sized pebble with one broken, but blunted edge. He placed the oval piece on his lap, and struck it with the other stone. It fell neatly into two halves, exposing the blue black hard interior. Djo's heart jumped. This could work!

He turned the piece, and struck it again. At an angle, this time, splitting off a smaller chunk down through the stone. With a few strokes, he sliced away the white chalky coating, and was left with an uneven, roughly triangular shape of glassy smooth stone. It was an ugly shape. Dark and strange. But Djo could see beyond that. The angles spoke to him. They described something to him. Somewhere, buried deep in the translucent rock, was a weapon. A blade more powerful than anything his father, or anyone in the village had ever known. A weapon so strong, so sharp, so new that it could kill monsters.

He stared into the flint and he could almost see it. Heavy and thick, it hung in a strange, half-glimpsed space between the dark of Djo's mind, and the depths of the black stone.

He hefted it in one hand and started to strike rapidly around the edges with the other, chipping off crumbs of stone with his make-shift hammer. He chipped his way around the side of the stone in a gentle curve, forming a cutting edge.

He ran his thumb along it. It was sharp, but rough and delicate. No good as a weapon, but Djo knew he could fix that. He turned his hammer stone over and used its rough, rounded edge to grind against the blade, sanding away the rough edges and the chips, sharpening it into a single, smooth line.

He closed his eyes, and took himself back to the moment he had thrown his Firstblade. Felt the weight of it again, light in his hands. Felt it spin into the bear's chest. He froze the moment in his head, the blade entering the fur, and being slowed by it. The bear's great paw crashing onto the shaft of the spear, and his bone blade with its delicate sculpted edges cracking and falling into the mud. That was it. This new blade had to be thicker. Heavier. In his mind, he transformed the bone blade into the one he was making. It would feel heavier, but when it hit the fur, it would not stop, it would pierce deep. And when the bear's paw smashed down - he played that moment in his mind, allowing himself to feel every motion of it, feel the fear, the motion in his muscles, the impact.

He let those feelings shape his strikes into the stone. Not as knowledge, but as understanding, afeeling for where the blade should be sharp, where it should be heavy. Where it should be strong. The stone would need to be thin enough at the blade to slice through, but thick enough in the middle to hold. To let the bear's paw smash the shaft, but leave the blade stuck deeply and fatally in its chest. He let his feelings guide the motion of his hands.

Working feverishly now, he thinned the stone down, forming another cutting edge along the other side, and meeting them at a sharp, thick stabbing point. At the back, behind the blade, he flattened the stone, ready for it to be fixed firmly to a wooden spear.

When it was finished, he held it up to the light. It was a strange thing. A long, sharpened oval shape. It looked familiar. He had made something he had seen before. The chipped stone rippled like the sides of an iceberg, but it was not that.

It was the boat! The boat in which they had made their final escape from the orcas. Their first footstep in the land of monsters. The rounded blade was the long, sharp-fronted shape of their boat. Something in his mind had made him carve the outline of the boat they had built to take them home, but then used to cross to this new shore. A bridge between the old world and the new. It was right, somehow.

The sun glinted from the sculpted edges. He turned it in his fingers and light refracted through the blade, making it shine and glow at the same time. All blades had a power, of course. They were the knowledge of the village, its history and its future. They were death and life and everything depended on them. Everything came back to them.

But this one - this one seemed to have a dark spirit. Something powerful and dangerous. Alien materials sculpted by ideas nobody had ever had before, for an unimaginable purpose in a land no human had ever visited. He felt as if it were too much for him. As if he, a mere human, should not wield such a powerful thing. As if this blade had the power to transform this strange land. Destroy it, even.

The shaft was as important as the blade, his father had always told him. It had to tell the hunter's story, whatever that story was. Back home, it would have been a bone from a great kill, or a family gift. It would have been carved with patience and skill. But there was no time for that now.

He searched the forest floor, with no idea what he was looking for, discarding one stick after another, with no clear idea about why, or what he was looking for. And then he saw it. A stick, just the right thickness, straight and true. The length of his arm. But what spoke to him was the colour. The bark had been completely burned away in the fire, but somehow, the wood underneath was spared. Now the pale, blond bare wood was exposed. Swirled and stained with black smoke it was a complex and beautiful pattern, but it was more than that.

It spoke of his fears. His mistakes, but also his power. He regretted the fire, of course. It was wrong. To have arrived in this new land, and wreaked such destruction on it. It was wrong in a way that made his heart sick every second his eyes were open. But it was powerful too. The monsters here were huge and strange, but Djo had a power too. The power of knowledge. And it was time to take ownership of that power.

The blade made short work of the shaft, slicing its ends, cleanly, and splitting one so that he could wedge the stone into it. He bound it with twisted strands of grass, soaking them first in the river, and wrapping them over and over around the base of the blade.

Finally, he left the spear in the sun to dry. As the grasses dried, they would shrink, becoming tighter and stronger until the blade was firm and secure.

The type of stone knife Djo has just made is called a Clovis blade. It is similar to weapons found in the archaeological sites of ancient peoples all over America. At the time, it was the most technologically advanced weapon the human race ever had produced. It was thicker, sharper, and stronger than the weapons of Siberian humans (Djo's ancestors), and it was essential to man's attempts to survive amongst the monsters of America.

The Clovis blade is probably the most important artefact left by the mysterious first people to discover the New World. It could well have been key to their survival there. And those colonists did indeed transform the world they discovered beyond all recognition.

You can find out how to make a Clovis blade on YouTube.

Chapter 40

"I'm hungry!" It was Chi. She had awoken with no sign of her earlier tears. The leaf bandage was still over the cut on her hand, but she seemed to have forgotten it. It was as though sleep had erased the memory of the bear, and now all she could think of was her stomach.

"Me too!" said her brother, the words coming before he opened his eyes.

Djo felt it too. During the weeks on the iceberg with the rich, dark meat of the mammoth waiting for them at every sitting, the crispy, browning fat dancing and spitting in the fire as they huddled around it, their stomachs had forgotten hunger.

Now, it had returned, and Djo felt it as a physical pain. Whatever else happened, they had to eat.

The new weapon was there, its bindings drying on the rock, its blade eating light and returning it strangely changed, like something alive. Djo reached out and traced his fingers along its smoked grip. He lifted it slowly, testing its weight, feeling it for the first time, not as his creative work, but as a weapon. As a tool. It was heavy. He held it in the middle, the way he was taught, and it fell forwards.

It took most of his strength to keep the blade from sinking to the ground. In a few seconds, his hand started to ache from the strain of carrying it. It felt uncomfortable. Wrong.

"Follow me," he told the twins, "but quietly, and carefully."

The woods looked dead. Any animals here had fled or burned last night, but the river was wide and shallow here, and it had blocked the path of the fire. On the other side, the plain was a huge, empty grassland. Dry, yellow grasses matted over the brown dirt, and here and there, richer, greener grass grew in thick clumps like islands. The flat land stretched away, yellow to distant blue mountains. In places, trees stood alone, or in groups of two or three, and around them and between them, brown specks moved. The monsters.

As Djo picked his way from rock to rock across the clear, shallow river, with the twins leaping behind, he stopped to stare out over the`plain. It was familiar to him, but at the same time strange and, for the first time, he realised why. The plain was like, and at the same time completely unlike the scrubland of home. It was the same wide, flat open ground, only warmer, brighter, and infinitely more full of life. Back home the grass was patchy and brittle against hard frosted ground. The trees were rarer, smaller. They were windswept and mostly leafless sticks like fingers of mud rising out of the ground. And the creatures. At home, you could wander for days without seeing another creature. Here, huge animals crowded the horizon. They strode between grass patches. They sheltered under trees.

Home. Djo caught himself. He had to stop thinking of the village as home. Whatever the future held for he and the twins, one thing was certain: he would never see the village again. He had come too far, and there was no way back. But the feeling was buried deep inside him. Whenever the village, his father, the elders popped into his head, whenever this land reminded him that it was like, or not like home, it was like a punch in the stomach. It weakened him. It slowed his legs, and crowded his mind, and that risked all of their lives.

And when he thought of Di, it was worse. He could control his thoughts of home, put them off until they could grab a few moments of safety, with food and fire, and shelter around them. But Di - the way Djo felt right now, it would never be safe to think of her again.

He scooped a handful of river water, and splashed it over his face, hoping the cold shock would clear his mind. Over to his left, in the distance, a herd of thick-necked beasts grazed. He could pick out horns sticking up above the grasses, and there were too many to count.

Chapter 41

Djo and the twins reached the other side, and he led them into the grass. He wasn't hunting monsters. Right now, he just needed enough food to keep the twins quiet.

Rabbits. He could see them already, two, no three of them, sitting, munching on a clump of grass just up ahead. He told the twins to keep low and quiet as he circled round and settled to watch his prey.

Back home, rabbits were thin and nervous things. Scavenging lichen and hard leaves, they hugged the ground as they sprinted between icy burrows, ribs scraping the frost. You had to be fast and launch your spear the moment you saw a movement.

Here, things were different. The rabbit just a few paces away from him was plump and healthy. Djo watched it sitting in the sun, chewing slowly. Its ears flicked. Slowly, it turned its head towards him. He froze. The rabbit stared straight at him for a few seconds, then continued chewing, unconcerned. He watched it and, after finishing its mouthful, it actually hopped closer to him in search of greener grass.

The creature had obviously never seen a human before. To the rabbit, he was just another part of the landscape. The least threatening animal in a land filled with monsters. He wondered how long it would take them to learn as he slowly lifted the spear, hauling it back behind his shoulder, ready to launch. He struggled to level it, his wrist fighting against the weight of the heavy tip. It felt unbalanced. Awkward. But its blade hovered at the edge of his vision, black and shining in the space to the left of his ear.

He took a low silent breath, tensed and propelled the spear forwards. As his body turned, and his shoulder followed through, the rabbit glanced up in alarm, but it was too late. The arrow was already in flight.

Djo knew something was wrong instantly it left his fingers. The spear wobbled, pitched forwards, and tipped, clattering into the earth in front of the rabbit, then spinning over it and somersaulting, twisting harmlessly to the ground. The rabbit bolted and, in a second, so did its companions. Djo cursed to himself. None of them would ever let a human get that close again.

"You missed," said Cha.

"Yes," said Djo. "I missed."

"Why did you do that?"

"I didn't mean to," he said. "The spear - it - "

"But I'm hungry!" insisted Cha.

"Me too," said Chi.

"We're all hungry!" said Djo, picking up the spear, furious with it, and with himself.

"You're not a very good hunter," said Cha.

"I wish Ra and Di were here instead," said Chi. "They're good hunters."

"Well, they're not here!" said Djo.

"When are they coming back?" said Chi.

"They're gone," said Djo. "They're not coming back ever! They've left you. It's just me now." He stalked off through the grass, leaving the twins staring at each other, wide-eyed.

Behind him, he heard them pause and then run after him. He felt awful.

"But I'm hungry. What am I going to eat?" Djo didn't even know which one had said it, but both of them were starting to cry. He spun around.

"I'm doing my best," he shouted, shoving the spear into his belt.

They stared back at him. He wanted to yell at them until they stopped complaining. Until they understood how bad things were. He opened his mouth. Then he saw Chi. Her lip trembled. There were tears in her eyes. Now he just wanted to hug them both and tell them everything would be all right.

Instead, something else caught his eye. Back at the river, a dark brown shape was moving, sniffing at the ground where they had been sleeping just a few minutes before.

Chapter 42

The bear turned its huge head, and rose up on two legs, staring out over the river and across the grassland towards them. For a second, Djo met its cruel eyes.

"Run!" he shouted.

The twins turned and followed his gaze. The bear crashed onto all fours and bounded into the river. Spray erupted around it. The twins started to run, arms flailing as they leapt over and through the grasses. Djo followed.

"Head for the tree!"

Up ahead, an old broad trunked tree spread out its boughs wide to catch the sun. Around it, a few shrubs were scattered. Djo wasn't sure what he would do if they made it to the tree, but the grassland was wide and open. There was nothing else.

He looked back. The bear had cleared the river already. Unlike the ice bears, its legs were long, designed for running. The monster galloped, more like a deer than a bear, its mouth hanging open, exposing those vicious teeth. It was so fast. With every step it was getting closer.

Djo ran past the twins, stooping to scoop them up, one in each arm. He staggered forward, forcing himself on. He was trying to leap over lumps of grass, but the weight of the two children in their still wet clothes was pulling him down.

His own fur jacket was thick and heavy too. His boots were caked in mud and soaked through from the river, and he fought against them, with every step.

The tree was closer now. In its shade, he could see the lowest, thickest boughs. As he ran on, he planned his route up the tree, a leap to the lowest branch, a stretch with one arm to grab a higher one and pull himself up. A well-timed swing into the higher branches. He could do it. Chi and Cha would have to make their own way up, but they were better climbers than he was. The question was, could the bear climb too?

He staggered forward, half running, half toppling towards the tree. He could feel his heart thumping in his chest. The sweat pouring down his back and chest. He couldn't even use his arms to run, the twins were so heavy they nearly pulled him off balance as he tried to find a rhythm to make running easier.

He looked around. The bear was closer than ever now, eating up the ground between them. This was its land. Its legs were made for this landscape. Its body for this heat. Djo's was made for the ice. He turned back, and struggled on.

The tree was close now, but his lungs were burning. He was gasping for breath, and his arms felt so heavy they were almost numb. As he entered the shadow of the tree, he could almost feel the breath of the creature on his neck, almost smell it. In his mind, he could see those jaws. They would be at the height of his own head. He imagined them spreading wide just behind him, twisting forward to envelope his skull.

With one last leap, he stepped up onto the low hanging bough, and hurled Chi and Cha forward and up into the higher branches. They grabbed instinctively and scrambled away from him as he caught the higher branch and used his own forward momentum to swing his legs high onto the next branch. As he flipped over and upwards, he caught a glimpse behind him. The bear was leaping. Just an arm's length away, its mouth was open, its eyes fierce. Its great paws reached out towards him.

He reached out blindly above him, fumbling for the next branch. For a second, he felt nothing. Then his fingers caught a feathery handful of twigs, and he grasped hard, pulling himself into the tree. He felt them crack, and start to tear away, and his other hand flew out to grip another, stronger branch, even higher.

In a second he was out of the creature's reach. Below him, it reached up, on two legs, roaring its fury. It batted the tree, trying to grip. Its long claws hooked into the bark, and it started to haul itself off the ground. Its back legs were on the lower branch now, and it forced its head up through the higher branches towards them. Suddenly, it scrabbled clumsily, and fell back, crashing to the ground. Its pure bulk made it impossible for it to hold on. Unlike the ice bears, this creature was no climber.

Chapter 43

Djo looked up. Chi and Cha were in the upper branches already. Chi was staring down, wide eyed and silent. Even Cha was clinging on to his branch, too scared to move.

"Hang on, I'm coming up," said Djo. But as he started to move, he realised that the bear had not given up.

The entire tree suddenly shuddered. He looked down. Through the branches, he could see the bear. It was standing high on its back legs. Its paws were held out in front of it facing the tree. As Djo watched, it tilted forward, crashing into the trunk with its great paws. Another massive shockwave rippled up to the top branches. Above him, Chi screamed. Djo looked up. She was hanging from the underside of her branch, arms and legs wrapped around it. She hugged it with all her strength, desperately clinging on as the tree shook again.

Now the bear grabbed the trunk below them, digging its claws deep into the bark on each side of the tree. It swung back, using all the power in its back legs, pulling the trunk back. The tree moved only gently. The bear pushed back, swaying the tree again as though in a gentle breeze.

Djo started to climb up towards where Chi was hanging, but below him, the bear was pulling the tree again, this time, aided by the natural spring of the trunk, it swung a little further. The bear pushed, finding the tree's rhythm, and pulling and pushing in time with it, slowly building the strength of its swing.

By the time Djo got to the branch below Chi, the whole tree was shaking wildly, swinging back and forth in an ever widening arc. Chi was screaming over and over now, hanging from the underneath of the branch. Djo watched as her hands started to slip on the bark. Her feet unlocked from around it, and she hung by her arms for a second before letting go completely.

Without thinking, Djo leapt from his branch to catch her. He grabbed her around the waist and they both fell. Djo felt the branches crashing past his face, scratching in a blur of green and brown. His back struck a branch, and he felt it snap under him. He shut his eyes tight, waiting to smash into the ground, but suddenly, the fall slowed to a bouncing halt. Underneath him, he felt a soft mat of leaves. He opened his eyes. The broken branch had somehow become snagged on a lower bough, its wide spread of leaves formed a nest underneath them, holding them, just. He turned his head and peered down. The bear was close. Its head, almost touching distance below him, starred up. For a moment, Djo locked eyes with it. Sharp and clever, it seemed to be looking right into his mind. "You gave me your sister," it seemed to be saying. "What will you give me now?"

Djo wrenched his eyes away, but the bear was still shaking the tree. The trunk swayed impossibly, first one way, then the other. The trunk was bending so much that at the outer edges of the canopy, leaves scraped the ground. With each swing, Djo felt his insides wrench first one way and then the other. His head swooped with dizziness. And at the edges of each swing, as the movement changed direction, they had to hang on to prevent themselves being thrown out onto the ground. There were sounds now, too. Terrifying, dangerous creaking cracking sounds coming from the trunk as it swung back and forth. How much more could it take?

From above, there was a cry, and Cha plummeted down, shaken loose to crash into the mat of leaves next to Djo and Chi. There was a crack. The whole branch shifted. It was balanced, now on a tangled web of twigs in the branch below, swinging like a hammock. It could give way at any second.

Djo looked down through the branches as they swung back and forth. The bear was right there below him, looking up as it hauled the cracking tree back and forth, the blood of the monster at the riverside still soaked on its face and hands.

There was one chance. Djo pulled the heavy spear from his belt and angled it down through the leaves. Branches were in his face. The tree was swinging in sickening swoops. His arm was bent back so he was at the wrong angle for a strong throw, but perhaps if he struck downwards at the creature's face?

He measured the distance, as the tree slowed at the end of its swing, and drove the blade down with all his strength.

But the bear was too quick. It dodged, and brought its claw up, batting at the spear, wrenching it from Djo's hand, and sending it spinning to the ground where it stuck, blade deep into the dirt.

Djo's heart sank. That was it. He had failed. It was his one shot, and he had messed it up. And now for the second time that day, he had lost his only weapon to the bear.

The bear roared back up the tree at him, and crashed down onto all fours. It had been forced to let go of the tree to bat the spear away, and the swinging slowed to a stop. The bear looked at the tree trunk, then up at Djo in the branches. Something in its eyes suggested to Djo that it was thinking. Calculating whether the work it would take to start the tree shaking again was worth the scrawny lumps of meat hanging in it. It swung its head towards the tree, and then away. It paced around the trunk. Finally, it simply slumped down into a sitting position, back against the tree.

It had decided to take the easy route, and simply wait for them to come down.

Chapter 44

"What are we going to eat?" said Cha.

They had been sitting in the tree for a couple of hours by now, and a red dusk was settling over the plain. Djo had watched strange animals come and go but the bear had not moved. Cunning and patient, it knew they had no way out, and all it had to do was wait.

The tree did have fruits. Purple ovals about the size of his palm. The children wanted meat, of course, but the fruit looked edible. Djo grabbed one piece, and bit into it. It was sweet and juicy. He handed it to Cha. The little boy snatched it, and stared at it. He took a bite.

"I hate you." he said, munching on the fruit. "This isn't food." Djo handed a fruit to Chi. She took it, but she wasn't even looking at it. She was staring down at the base of the tree where the monster was sitting, waiting to devour them.

The children were right. How could he have even thought they could survive. He had held the most powerful weapon anyone could possess, and he had failed even to kill a rabbit from three paces away.

It was all over, Djo thought. The day was ending, and they would never survive the night.

As the light faded, he watched it dim, and all the strength left in his body faded too. His stomach felt empty, but it wasn't a hunger anymore. Hunger is the hope of food, and hope was gone now. There was just the emptiness. He didn't even bother to eat the fruit. What was the point?

Djo put his head in his hands and started to sob. Ra and Di had been right. Ra had been right to say the things he had said, and Di had been right to lead him off into the forest. To abandon them. He and the twins were the weak ones. She must have seen that. And in a world like this, the weak did not survive. He had been angry with her at first, but that feeling was gone now too, and he was just left with a desperate sadness. He understood. She was right. If it hadn't been for the fire, she and Ra would have stood more chance without Djo and the children slowing them down. They were going to die anyway. Why should Di and Ra die too? She had done what she had to do and in a way, she was being kind. Her grandmother would have been proud of her.

Djo watched the light die, and the moon start to glow white. Below him, the shape of the bear glowered at the bottom of the tree, a dark, blurry smudge of shadow, deeper than the shadow of the earth.

The shape moved. It hauled itself up, and turned around to face the tree once more, peering up into the branches. In the night, its body was one single hulking darkness, but its eyes reflected the moon. They stood out, sharp and cruel, staring into Djo's, hypnotising him. "I am everything you have done," it seemed to say. "I am the frozen fear that stopped you saving Leal. I am the guilt that your friend Rhor took your place on the hunt and died in your place. You ran from the mammoth, and took the children out onto the ocean, and now, without its children, the whole village will die. You burned the forest and killed your friends. You created me. I am your guilt. Your fear. Your failings. I am the hunter and you are my prey."

Djo watched. Perhaps it was hungry. Perhaps it was just bored of waiting, but the bear started to shake the tree again. This time, there was no hesitation. No uncertainty. It knew the strength of the trunk. It knew the rhythm that would eventually break it. The bear set to its work with a slow, deliberate motion. Back and forth. Back and forth, and slowly the tree began to sway.

This was it, thought Djo. Finally, this was the end. There was nothing to fight the bear. Nothing to distract it. Nothing to scare it off. A part of him was glad. Soon it would all be over.

And then he felt Cha's hand reach out for his, and the brave little boy wrapped his arms around Djo, clinging to him so tightly it hurt. "Is it going to eat us?" he said.

Chapter 45

Djo grabbed both of them, and pulled them to him. He couldn't let this happen. Not after everything they had been through. Not after the iceberg and the orcas and the fire. How could he just give up? They had survived all that and whatever the voice in his head told him, they had survived it because of him.

Djo fumbled in the bag at his belt. He had one thing. His bow and spindle. His fire-making tools. His father's words came back to him: "The bear fears only fire."

But how could he use it? How could he dare after what happened last time?

No choice. The swinging of the tree was getting stronger.

He placed the spindle against a dent in the tree's dry bark, and started to spin it with the bow. In seconds, it began to smolder. The voice inside was telling him how foolish this was. How stupid. The tree was the only thing between him and the bear, and the only cover in sight. And he was setting it alight. If it caught, they would have to come down, or be burnt alive. What if the bear just stepped back and waited for them to be smoked out? What if the rest of the grassland caught fire? What if the flames caught their clothing?

Even if by some miracle, the bear withdrew from the flames, it would only be a matter of time before it came back, and then they would have nowhere to hide.

Still, he continued to twist the spindle, tearing hairs from his coat with his other hand and, grabbing a few dry twigs and bark fragments. He scrunched the furs and leaves into a tight ball.

By now, the tree was swaying more strongly with each swing. The twins were clinging on, but Djo couldn't. He had to use both hands to hold the spindle in place as he spun it. He braced his shoulder against the trunk, and hooked his feet into the tangle of branches beneath him, hoping they would hold as he tried to keep his balance.

Orange fragments of dust were starting to fall from the spindle now, glowing for a second then drifting and fading as they fell into the darkness. Djo held his ball of hair and twigs under the spindle to catch the sparks, and then, dropping the bow and spindle down through the branches, he cradled the ball in both hands. He heard his fire-lighting tools clatter down the trunk to the ground as he held the ball to his lips, blowing into the tiny specks of ember, coaxing them into life while the world swayed around him.

This had to work. It was their only chance.

The ball of fur and twigs glowed and smouldered a little. He smelled the smoke in his nose. Then the light at the centre of the ball started to dim. He blew again, over and over into the darkening heart of his hands. He was starting to feel dizzy now, partly from the swinging of the tree, partly from the deep gulps of smoky air he was taking.

Suddenly, the handful of dark smoke and hair ignited from the inside. In a second, he was holding a ball of fire.

Quickly, he pressed it against the tree trunk, and the dry, wrinkled bark of the old tree smoked, sparked, and then caught alight. Flame ran up the side of the tree like a climbing animal running for its life.

When they reached the top, the flames fanned out and leapt in a tall cone above the tree, circling the highest, thinnest branches, and throwing flickering light down onto the children, and the monster below them.

Djo looked down. The bear's eyes reflected the flame, furious and blazing. It paused for a second, paws still gripped around the trunk. Djo grabbed a thin branch, snapped it off, and plunged its leaves into the fire above him. It caught instantly, and he turned it and shoved it down between the branches, dropping it onto the creature's back.

The bear let go of the tree and fell onto all fours. It twisted and shook itself, trying to dislodge the burning branch on its back. In a second, the branch had fallen off, but a patch of fur was glowing now. The creature howled in pain, then it rolled over onto its back and rubbed the burning patch into the dusty ground. In a second, it was out.

The bear turned, looked Djo straight in the eyes, and roared, its huge yellow teeth shining in the flame and the moonlight. Then it turned to look up at the flaming tree.

It stared for a second, and then backed slowly away out of the circle of firelight and into the darkness beyond, glaring up at Djo as it retreated. Djo stared after it. A cold fear gripped him. The bear's message was clear. It was not turning and running from the fire like an ice bear would have, it was withdrawing, eyes locked on its prey. "This is not over," it was saying. "You will have to come down, and I will be waiting. I am the moments that made you and I will be there at your end."

Chapter 46

Above them, the top of the tree was a roaring funnel of flame. The burning embers of leaves were falling all around them in a glowing rain of fire. Each leaf curled, blackened and disintegrated as it fell, and the smell of sweet sticky fruit cooking on its boughs mixed with the smell of smoking wood.

Heat was creeping down from the top of Djo's head as the fire ate the tree from the top down. Already, he could feel his face blushing red. The twins cowered under his coat.

They had maybe five minutes before it became unbearable, and forced them down into the circle of light, and then eventually out into the darkness where the monster waited.

Djo peered out into the blackness. Maybe there was another tree, or something he had not spotted before. He shaded his eyes from the fire, and let them adjust to the silvery light of the moon. The plain stretched away to the mountains, visible now only as a zig-zagging gap in the thick speckling of stars. Below them and closer, there were shades in the darkness, but Djo couldn't tell now whether they were trees, wandering monsters or just tricks of the darkness.

In the other direction, he could just make out the pale shine of the moon on the river. He knew there was nothing closer that way.

The heat was burning now. A lowering wall, pushing down on them from above. Chi and Cha huddled close to him. They would have to take the chance. Run into the blackness and hope that by some miracle there was something out there.

"Come on," he said to Chi and Cha. "We have to go."

They stared at him, wide-eyed with fear. They knew as well as he did that this was suicide. Djo hooked his legs over his branch ready to swing himself down to the ground. He took one last look out back towards the river.

And suddenly there was something there in the distance. Two orange lights. They bobbed like sparks on the plain. Up and down. Up and down. Djo stared at them. Two little fires. Torches. And they were coming closer.

Chapter 47

Di and Ra! They were alive! They must have seen the burning tree and realised it could only be Djo's work.

"Run!" he shouted.

The two torches bobbed faster, growing. Pools of light spread around them, illuminating the grass in a yellow glow. Two faces. It was them.

Without even thinking, Djo was out of the tree. His knees buckling as he hit the ground, he staggered, stumbled and steadied himself, running headlong towards Di. He threw his arms around her, suddenly, unexpectedly sobbing.

With everything that had happened, he had pushed her to the edges of his mind. Now, suddenly all the feelings he had been holding under himself rose up in his stomach and took over his body. It was relief, hope, tiredness, fear, all rolled into one, and maybe something else too.

"I thought you were dead!" he managed.

"We went to get food," said Ra. He pulled a stick from his belt. Five plump rabbits were tied to it. He dumped them on the ground.

"- and then there was the fire," said Di. Then she added, quietly, "I thought you were dead too." She touched his face. Her eyes were wet with tears.

"I thought you'd left us!" said Djo, squeezing her.

"Never!" she said.

"But I thought," said Djo, "you and Ra-" Di put her finger to his lips to stop him. When she took it away, he could still feel its imprint there. She smiled, and a second later, he felt her lips against his in a kiss that silenced all his doubt.

"Where are the twins?" she said.

"They're-" he turned. Chi and Cha were clambering out of the burning tree, running towards them. Di smiled. She crouched down to gather them into her arms.

Djo turned to Ra. The scar on his face from their fight was still red. He nodded at it. "I'm sorry," he said. Ra held up his hand to stop Djo.

"Doesn't matter," Ra said. "I'll get you next time." But there was something in his voice. Something softer.

"We can't stay here," said Djo.

"I know" said Ra. "There's a monster - a giant bear-"

"It's here," said Djo. "It's after us!"

Instantly the two hunters drew their spears and spun to face away from Djo and the twins, protecting them. Ra thrust his torch into Djo's hands.

"Back under the tree!" barked Ra. "Stay close!"

The group moved back under the tree, forming a tight circle, spears and torches pointing outward. The heat was almost unbearable, and burning leaves were raining all around them, but at least they could see a few paces all around them. If the bear came - when the bear came, they would at least see it coming.

"We ran into it in the forest," said Di.

"After you'd burnt it down," added Ra.

"Ra tried to spear it," said Di.

"and?" said Djo.

Ra shook his head. "Spears are no good," he said. "It's too fast. Too strong. I drove it off though - just."

"We were lucky," added Di. "That other monster - the one from the beach came past us. The bear followed it down to the river."

The light of the flaming tree cast flickering shadows at the edge of the circle of light. The darkness seemed to be in constant life, just at the edge of vision. It was out there somewhere, watching.

"That's when we met it," said Djo. "It took my Firstblade. Snapped it in pieces."

Ra was staring at him, open-mouthed.

"I know it wasn't the best blade -" Djo started.

"What do you mean?" said Ra. "Your blade was..." - he was struggling for words- "...amazing!"

Djo looked at him in disbelief. "You said it was rubbish," said Djo.

Ra looked away, scanning the shadows.

"I know what I said," Ra couldn't look at him. "But you're the best blademaker in the village. It's all the elders talk about."

"Not to me," said Djo, staring out into the dark, his eyes beginning to well up again. Because of the smoke, he told himself.

"You mean you never knew?" said Ra.

"I thought you just hated me," said Djo.

Ra stared at him now, amazed.

"Of course I hated you - you were the best at everything," said Ra, still not making eye contact. "All I could do was fight and throw."

Djo swallowed. He couldn't believe what he was hearing. This was his enemy. The boy who had threatened to kill him - tried to kill him. Was this all out of jealousy? It was as though everything Djo knew about the world was shifting. Ra was the hero - he always had been. How could Ra be jealous of Djo?

"Without you we'd be dead," said Djo.

"You'd have survived," said Ra. "Back on the iceberg I was ready to give up - you were the one who saved us." Djo coughed, holding back the tears.

"Doesn't matter, now, does it? The blade is broken," he said.

Chapter 48

Out on the edge of the circle of light, Djo could swear he saw movement. A darker shape in the darkness, stalking back and forth just beyond the range of certain vision. He couldn't make out a head or legs, just a huge bulk, lurking in the shadows, back and forth, back and forth, waiting for its moment.

"What's this?" said Ra, suddenly. He was looking at the ground to one side of the tree, where Djo's dark stone blade with its ash-marked shaft was sticking out of the ground. He stepped forward, and pulled it out of the earth, turning it upright to examine the glittering blade.

"I tried to make a spear," said Djo. "It's useless." He went back to focusing on the shifting shadows at the edge of the light.

"It's beautiful," said Ra, turning it in the firelight.

"It doesn't work," said Djo, snatching it from him. He held it up to demonstrate, grasping it in the middle. The heavy blade drooped. "See - too heavy. It won't even fly straight."

Ra grabbed the weapon, and felt its balance. The tip pitched forward, its weight pulling it towards the ground. Ra smiled.

"See," said Djo.

"Huh," said Ra, thoughtfully. He touched the blade, testing it with this thumb. Blood. Ra rubbed his fingers together, smearing it over them. "This is powerful," he whispered.

"No good if it won't fly," said Djo. At the edge of the light, the shadow had stopped pacing. Its shape was still, hunched.

"There!" said Djo, and at that moment, the bear burst out of the darkness, huge and terrifying.

On all fours, leaping forward, mouth gaping wide. Searing rage in its eyes. Djo shoved the torch forward into its face, and the beast stopped, rearing up onto its hind legs, bellowing. Behind him, he could feel the heat of the fire on his back. The twins cowered against the tree. Di stepped forward and jabbed with her spear.

The bear batted it with one huge paw, pushing it away. Di hung on, but was twisted to one side, almost losing her balance. The bear took a step forward, raising its other paw ready to bring down on Djo.

He thrust the flaming torch forward again. There was a crackle. The smell of burning hair. But the bear did not recoil. Instead, it twisted forward, pressing the torch into its body, and extinguishing it against itself.

Djo tossed the now useless torch on the ground. He was unarmed. He stared up into the animal's enraged face. It glared down. Three times his height.

To his left, Di spun back, jabbed again, hitting the distracted creature in the side, forcing it back for a second.

Djo looked for a weapon. Anything he could use. Beside him, Ra thrust Djo's own spear into his hands. Djo stared back. Why?

Ra was still staring at the flint blade, weighing it in his hands, almost hypnotised by it. As though he had not even noticed the monster facing them.

Ra's eyes widened in sudden realisation. "You were holding it wrong," he said. He shifted his hand up towards the blade until the spear rested easily there.

But the bear was coming again. This time slower, steadier, more certain. It was watching. Clever eyes switching from Djo to Di to the points of the spears and back. Watching each movement, slowly edging in, planning its strike. One swipe of its claws and it would all be over. It advanced, swinging its long arms in front of it, judging its moment. Suddenly, with one sweep, it knocked both spears to the side, then stepped in close enough for Djo to smell its stinking breath. It rose up ready to smash down with both paws on Djo and Di.

And in that second, Djo felt something fly past his head. Something heavy and dark and sure.

Chapter 49

The stone spear was in perfect, silent flight. As it passed his ear, the orange fire from above glinted on the rippled edge of the blade where Djo had struck to flake and sharpen it.

There was a thud, and a second's silence. The blade hit hard, sinking deep into the thick flesh around the bear's back leg. It froze, and then turned, bellowing and bounding away, spear still hanging from the wound in its thigh.

Djo turned. Ra was smiling. "You were holding it wrong. You have to find its balance," he said, "not force it to yours. You have to throw from near the head."

Outside the firelight, the bear roared in pain and anger. The sound tore through the night, and then died away. Ra's smile died with it. Djo looked out into the night. Perhaps the creature had fled, or keeled over and died.

But a part of him knew otherwise. The spear wound was deep and serious, but it was not fatal, and even in the moment after the spear struck, when the monster was fleeing, he had seen its eyes, and heard its voice. It feared nothing.

Suddenly a new sound came. From behind them this time. A creaking, splintering sound. Djo spun around in time to see the tree's thick trunk splitting only an arm's length above his head. The flaming branches pitched forward towards them. Djo grabbed the twins and threw them out from under the falling tree, then dived, his shoulder against Di's, propelling them both away from the crashing fire. They sprawled to the ground, and Djo turned in time to see Ra diving to one side as a red, glowing branch shattered into embers where he had been standing.

The trunk followed a fraction later, landing with a thud that shook the ground, and a rain of dancing, floating sparks, followed by an eye-watering wash of thick, dark smoke that made him screw up his eyes as they all struggled to their feet.

For a moment, there was no sound. The children cowered together. Then the smoke rose, and the bear's face appeared at the edge of the smouldering tree. Dark and slow, it stalked around the burning tree, back and forth, eyes locked on Djo. The spear still stuck out of its back leg, blood soaking the hair around its blade. "It is your time," it seemed to say inside his head.

"What do we do now?" said Djo. "The spear was all we had."

Ra gritted his teeth. "There's only one way," he said, grimly.

"What?" said Djo.

"You know - you're the clever one," said Ra. "We have to get the spear back."

Djo swallowed. Ra was right. There was no other way. But the spear was sticking out of the bear's side.

Whoever pulled it out would never survive. "I should go," said Djo.

"No," said Ra. He nodded at the others. "They can survive without me. They can't survive without you."

Djo stared at him. He couldn't believe Ra would say that.

"You don't understand," said Djo. "It's me it wants."

"What are you talking about?" said Ra.

Djo took a breath. It was time to confess.

"When the ice-bear took Leal, I was there," he said. The tears welled up in his eyes. His throat was tight with them. He could hardly speak. "I could have saved her. I could have shouted for help. I could have let it take me instead. But I didn't. I was too scared." Djo's breath came in short gasps. Finally, he had told them. Finally they knew who he really was. Waves of emotion swept over him.

Ra didn't move. "I know," he said. "I've always known. I was there too. I was standing by the huts. I saw it all."

Djo stared in disbelief. "Why didn't you do something?"

Ra shook his head. "Everybody gets scared," said Ra. "Even me. If it wants anybody, it wants me."

"No!" said Djo.

Ra didn't answer. Instead, he took one look back at Di, then nodded towards Djo and the twins.

"Look after them," he said, and then launched himself straight towards the bear. He dodged one way, then the other to avoid its claws, then as the monster turned, he grabbed the spear, and wrenched it out of the animal's side.

The bear roared, and spun its whole body around, its paw catching Ra and hurling him out into the darkness, the spear spinning from his grip. The bear followed, bounding out of sight after him.

Djo stepped forward, ready to follow. Di caught his arm and pulled him back.

Sounds came from the darkness. Roaring. Tearing. Ra cried out. There was a crash, and another, a noise which could have been snapping sticks, but wasn't.

Suddenly, the spear came flying out of the night and thudded into the ground at Djo's feet. He stared at it. Ra had found the spear, but he hadn't used it. The bear must have been too close for him to throw it. And instead of trying to save himself, he'd thrown it to Djo.

"Take it," said Di. "It's yours."

Djo reached down. His mind spinning. How could he have been so wrong about Ra? All his life he had thought that Ra hated him. That all the older boy cared about was himself. But it wasn't true. Everything Ra had ever done had been to protect Djo and the twins. Ra had seen what had happened to Leal, and yet he had never hated Djo. He had just been jealous. Jealous of Djo's skills. Jealous of Di's feelings for Djo. How could he have got it all so wrong?

Djo grasped the spear, and pulled it up out of the ground. The bear was coming now. Leaping out of the darkness, its whole huge body in the air, like a mammoth in flight. A wall of muscle and fur and claws and teeth. Those wild, staring eyes, hurtling towards him.

Djo drew back the spear, holding it close to the blade. "Find its balance." It was Ra's voice in his head this time. Djo held his breath, focused himself, and flung the spear into the heart of the blackness just below those eyes and gaping jaws.

Chapter 50

The bear didn't taste good, but they roasted slices over the dying embers of the tree. The deep purple, red meat was fatty and tough, but it was the only meal they had eaten for days, and to kill without eating was wrong, monster or not.

By the time the tree had burnt itself out, daylight had come again in a pale blue light which spread from the sea. Djo wondered if the light would have struck their old home in the village before it hit them, but for the first time, the memory was not a sad one. The village was there. They were here. That was just how it was now. In a few minutes, it lit the tops of the mountains at the other side of the plain, then spread down, racing across the grassland to meet them as the sun rose.

When it was light enough, they recovered Ra's body and wrapped it so that the twins did not have to see the scars. Between them, Di and Djo carried it in silence back across the river, and up to the outcrop of rock where they had first looked out across the plain only a day ago.

They buried him in the shade of the rock where they had made their first camp, and with him they laid his own spear, and in his hands, they placed the new flint weapon too.

Now he knew how, Djo could make more blades. He would teach Di. He would even teach the twins. It would not be hard. But it was Ra who had first shown them how to use the new spear, and it seemed right to bury the first weapon with him.

Once they had covered him, deep enough that nothing would find the body for a thousand years, Djo and Di sat on the rock. While Cha and Chi played in the charcoal of the woodland behind them, the couple watched the herds of strange creatures on the plain.

There would be more monsters, Djo knew it. Maybe even more bears. But, now he knew they could survive here after all. He reached out a hand to touch Di's fingers. She let him for just a second before she pulled away.

"Enough of the soppy stuff," she said. "We'd better get started."

"Started with what?" said Djo.

"Somebody's got to teach you to hunt," she said. "You're rubbish."

One of the oldest discoveries of human burial in America is of a child who died around 12,700 years ago in Montana. The child was buried with a collection of Clovis blades just as Ra was. Nobody knows why, and certainly the child in that case was far too young to have been part of a hunt. However, it does suggest that the idea of burying the dead with weapons had somehow become important to the early settlers.

The journey of Djo and his friends and their discovery of America is just a story, and we don't know exactly how the first settlers came to arrive there. Here are a few of the problems scientists will find with the story:

1. Although nobody has yet found blades similar to the one Djo made, in Siberia, even though they are found all over America, it's not known exactly why these new weapons were created. It's possible they helped settlers tackle the huge new animals they found in America but we don't really know.

2. It's unlikely that the settlers would have developed their new weapons only one day after first arriving, but that's the kind of choice you make when you want to make a story more exciting.

3. Bears can climb trees better than humans. Although most bears are very good at climbing, the short-faced bear in our story was different. It was bigger, and heavier than modern bears and its legs were much longer. It was built for running, not climbing. It's likely that the short-faced bear would have been much less able to climb trees than the bears of today.

4. Icebergs are a very unusual way for people to travel. It's more likely that they would have journeyed over a much longer time, in small boats working their way along the coastline in small jumps.

5. It would take more than the five people in Djo's group to start a whole new country. Even if Di and Djo had eventually gone on to have children, and those children had their own children with Cha and Chi, that's still only a small number of people. Scientists think you need about 160 people at least to start a new country. Maybe Djo's father and the rest of the village decided to follow their children, and arrived a few weeks later. Maybe other people also became stranded from different places, and they eventually met up.

Whatever the fate of the first visitors, we do know that after the first humans appeared in America, and started to spread, the monsters began to die out. The giant short-faced bears are gone now. The mammoths are gone. The giant armadillos, the glyptodonts, the ground sloths, the camels and the sabre-toothed cats have all been wiped out. Did humans cause the extinction? Was Djo's accidental burning of the forest just a taste of what his descendants would do with the new powerful weapon he created? Or was it simply the change in climate that saw the end of most of the great animals of the ice age? We don't know.

But if you go to America now, and you dig in the right places, you might still find a distinctive boat-shaped Clovis blade, chipped from flint, lying in the dirt.

And of course, you can find them on Ebay too...

I really hope you enjoyed this book.

If you did, please take a moment to put a review on **Amazon**, mention it on **social media**, or just **tell a friend**. It really helps to spread the word.

Thanks so much,
Christian Darkin
Author.

You can also email me directly at
christian@anachronistic.co.uk
Or tweet **@animateddad**
I'd love to hear from you.

Printed in Great Britain
by Amazon